Quill's Adventures

in Wasteland

John Waddington-Feather

Illustrated by Doreen Edmond

John Muir Publications

Santa Fe, New Mexico

First published 1986 by Feather Books, England

John Muir Publications, P.O. Box 613, Santa Fe, NM 87504

Second edition. First printing

Library of Congress Cataloging-in-Publication Data
Waddington-Feather, John, 1933-
    Quill's adventures in Wasteland / John Waddington-Feather. — 2nd ed.
    p.   cm.
    Summary: Quill Hedgehog and the Great Beyonders try to thwart a
treacherous alley cat's plan to exploit the land around Black Wood.
    ISBN 1-56261-016-3
    [1. Hedgehogs — Fiction. 2. Conservation of natural resources — Fiction.]
I. Title.
PZ7.W11375Quil   1991
[Fic] — dc20   91-20715
                                                                  CIP
                                                                  AC

Designer : Marcy Heller
Typeface : Trump Mediaeval and Hadriano Roman
Typesetter : Business Graphics
Printer : Banta Company

Distributed to the book trade by
W. W. Norton & Company, Inc.
New York, New York

To Sarah, Katherine and Anna,
for whom this tale was first told

Chapter 1

W inter had come again to Hedgehog Meadow. The leaves had left Oak Tree, where Quill lived, and the garden outside was settling into its winter sleep. It hadn't been touched for days; not since the last leaf had dropped and Quill had burned the final sweepings-up from autumn off his path. The borders looked dead, the lawn had a rough, unshaven appearance, and the few vegetables left outside to face the weather had an abandoned air about them. Overhead, the sky was grey; full to the brim with snow which a north-easter had been freezing all week. Quill had felt it coming and had retreated into the snuggery of his home, which he rarely left once the day drew in around tea-time.

Several years had passed since his adventure in the Great Beyond, which he still visited regularly to meet his friends. Every summer he would set off to see Horatio Fitzworthy, the gentlemanly cat who was also as fond of wandering as ever. Sometimes he'd travel as far as Mereful or Furtherland till autumn drew him back, to do the rounds of his special friends like Brushy Fox in the Wood, Flash Otter on Riverside, and Swoop Hawk in his lonely homestead on the moors near Wasteland. Then, friendly as ever, he'd drop in on his return to visit other animals in his own Domusland.

Of the Wastelanders, who'd played such an unpleasant part in Quill's first visit to the Great Beyond, no more had been heard until . . . until the beginning of this story. They had fled back to Wasteland, licking their wounds and staying well inside their own country. Without Mungo Brown, the treacherous alley cat who had led them into the Great Beyond, they were leaderless, and spent the next few years squabbling and rioting among themselves after the manner of all unhappy people. They'd learned nothing from their defeat in the Great Beyond. When there wasn't rioting in their filthy cities, there was civil war as leader after leader came and went, usually slipping off into a neighbouring land loaded with ill-gotten wealth, when the going became too rough. So their country remained as polluted and ungovernable as ever, and their towns and cities as dirty as the ones they had tried to build in the Great Beyond.

In fact, Wasteland was more derelict than it had ever been. There were more rats, more horrid towns, more slummy cities, more greedy folk—and more and more misery. Their lives were drab, filled with the monotony of work and the emptiness of boredom they called "leisure." Only their leaders kept any sort of order through the Black Jackets, bullies of the worst kind. These folk lived in the greatest comfort and kept their position simply because they were more greedy and ruthless than the others. They trained an army of spies who informed on the others—and, indeed, added a new word to our own language, "ratted."

So ignorant were they of life outside their own country, so unaccustomed to anything but the squalor of their own lives and their mean, little ways, that few of the Wastelanders would have departed had they had the chance. Perhaps the most dreadful thing was they had adapted so much to their awful city-life, they couldn't change and didn't want to.

2

None, of course, dared to return to the Great Beyond. The Great Beyonders had learned their lesson after that invasion by the rats under Mungo Brown. Since then, they had seen to it that their frontier with Wasteland was well guarded and patrolled by the folk living there. Swoop Hawk and the Marshfolk were always on the lookout in case any rats returned, but none came.

However, some rats did visit Domusland, where Quill lived. They came through Black Wood having crossed the Mystery Marshes on the northern side of Wasteland. Once you got to Black Wood, it was a short journey to Hedgehog Meadow!

Quill had heard rumours, only rumours mind, from the people living near Black Wood, that some Wasteland rats had settled in makeshift homes on the edge of the wood, travelling round the farms and hamlets trying to buy antiques or old family heirlooms from the simple countryfolk. They picked up what they could—and a bit more besides! The previous year, someone had told Quill they had even bought an old small-holding this side of the Mystery Marshes, on an escarpment called the Lyth; but Quill wouldn't believe that. He knew the rats were no farmers. They'd long ago lost all skills of tilling the land. Rumours always flew thick, anyhow, in that part of Domusland, especially when rabbitfolk got hold of them. He never believed seven-eighths of what rabbitfolk said. They were notorious gossipers.

Yet there had always been some rum folk in Black Wood. There were magpies, for instance; cheap, flashy folk who dressed in loud clothes and had voices to match. They had pretty sharp eyes—and practices, too. They were always eyeing other folks' property, then practiced their traditional craft—burglary! And living so near Wasteland, there was always a ready market for whatever they stole. The rats were only too keen to buy anything of value, especially antiques or old paintings. Such things had van-

Wasteland rats buying things of value
from Domuslanders

ished long ago from their own land, in the days when they considered anything old was of no value and chucked it out.

Times had changed, however, and the rich Wastelanders now tried to buy anything old or beautiful, for such things were lacking in their land. It wasn't that they understood beauty or treasured the old. It was simply that antiques were expensive and they liked to possess expensive things. They were great show-offs, and the more they could make each other envious the better they liked it. They simply enjoyed hurting and upsetting one another by any means. They were miserable folk, I can tell you!

What Quill did not know—and no rabbit had told him, they were like that, the rabbits—was that several Black Wood folk had mysteriously disappeared. Their homes and farmsteads had been bought by the rats and their land prepared for building, for holiday homes for the richer ratfolk. In particular, a huge, luxury bungalow had been built near the Spring Coppice; a monstrosity of a place which did its best—and succeeded—to tell anyone passing how rich its owner was, and how lacking in taste. It was guarded by an electric fence and ugly-looking rats who let nobody near. In the area of Spring Coppice itself there was an undue amount of coming and going, which, of course, the rabbitfolk saw, but kept to themselves when they'd been paid to keep their mouths shut for once.

None of this Quill was aware of as he spent the winter snoozing by his fireside or chatting with Dink Dormouse, who visited him occasionally, when he himself was not snoozing the winter out by his own fireside down the Dingle. It was on one of his visits, when the wind howled down the chimney and the first flakes of snow were already falling, that Dink mentioned to Quill what had happened the previous summer, when the hedgehog had been away in the Great Beyond.

They had eaten a meal of hot, buttered crumpets, buttered so lavishly in fact it ran down through the holes and made a golden pool on the plate. They washed them down with plenty of tea, drinking, not from the dainty china tea-service Quill's great-aunt Betsy had left him, but from the homely mugs ringed in blue. The tea nestled in the teapot and grew richer on the hearth by the minute. The wind howled in envy all the more as Quill threw an armful of logs on the fire. It skirled round the house trying to find some cranny in its oaken walls and spoil their chat with an icy draught; but it failed abysmally. The two animals settled down and nattered away, quite oblivious of the racket outside.

"Oh, aah," said Dink after a comfortable pause and a lick or two on his fingers to take away the excess butter. "Lots of things have been happening over the other side of the shire while you've been away . . . 'specially Black Wood way . . ."

Quill leaned back in his armchair and laid his head on the cushion behind him. His eyes were already half-closed, but he enjoyed Dink's slow talk, more for the way he spoke than for what he said. Dink had the slow drawl the Dorfolk had used for generations. There wasn't always what you might call meat in his speech, but there was plenty of gravy.

"And what sort of things have the Black Wooders been up to then, Dink?" asked the hedgehog distantly, tracing faces in the black beams overhead.

"Bad things," said Dink. Then, after a significant pause, "Terrible bad things. The place is crawling with Wastelanders . . ."

Quill opened his eyes wide and left off tracing one rather complicated bit of graining that had developed into an interesting face. His own face registered enough surprise. "Wastelanders?" he echoed. "Wasteland rats?"

"Aar!" said Dink. "Who else? Big, black rats what have been an' bought up acres of land Black Wood way. Planning to build houses an' factories all over the place, so I'm told. Magpies and squirrels 'ave been an' gone in with 'em. Gettin' folk to sell 'em their land as fast as they can. Payin' 'em anything they ask—an' givin' it to 'em as well. Folks can't sell their own birthrights fast enough. There's quite a packet of rats there now."

"No!" said Quill in disbelief. "Who's told you that?"

"The rabbitfolk . . ." began Dink.

"Rabbitfolk! You don't want to believe a word *they* say. They'll gossip about anything if they've the chance. Blow things out of all proportion. Don't believe a word of it!" said Quill brusquely.

Dink looked at Quill in the slow, hurt way he always looked when contradicted. Quill knew at once he'd been too hasty and apologised.

"That's all right," said Dink, continuing as if nothing had happened. "As I was saying, the rabbitfolk were gossiping about what had happened last year . . . last full moon twelve month to be exact . . . but no one took no notice. No one as matters anyways. But I had to go over to Black Wood this summer to see a cousin who'd fallen ill, Cousin Dorp, you know, who lived in Old Coppice, an' there it was—gone!"

"Gone? What was gone?" asked Quill, by now very agitated and a deal less comfortable.

"Spring Coppice an' the escarpment bramble patch. They cleared the lot an' built houses right across the hillside there . . . leastways, they've gone an' built this huge bungalow an' were making room for more."

"Never!" exclaimed Quill. "Here in our own shire, in Domusland? Why it's impossible! The Shire Moot there would never let them!"

"That's just it," said Dink. "It was the Black Wood Moot what asked 'em in. The Moot isn't what it was any more. All sorts of odd folk have gone an' gotten themselves put on the Moot that ought never have to have gone an' been putten there at all."

"What sort of folk?" asked Quill.

"Well, for a start the magpies and minkfolk. They've been voting themselves on the Shire Moot as fast as decent folk have disappeared. Now they're in control. That's what made my other cousin poorly. You remember Derry? Well, Dorp was ill, but Derry was poorly . . . proper poorly."

"Derry! I've never known your Derry ill in all his life," said Quill. "We went to old Bamber's school together as lads. I've known him all my life. Went over Black Wood way to work for one of the gentry, then bought his own little farm, didn't he?"

"That he did," said Dink. "An' worked hard to raise the cash for that farm he did. Nothing grand, mind. Just a little small-holding. But his all the same, an' he turned it into a nice farm with hard work. But they gone an' grabbed it off of him . . . an' that's what made him poorly . . . being grabbed!"

"Grabbed!" said Quill, his voice almost a whisper.

"Aar, grabbed," Dink repeated. "Thieved! The Shire Moot is so full of villains now, they're passing by-laws all the time so's they can bypass reg'lar laws an' grab folks' land. Once it's been grabbed, they start getting ready to build on it. An' there's something else the rabbitfolk told me. There's a fellow what's been made chairman or something of the Shire Moot, not more than a year ago, who's the rogue behind all this land-grabbing."

"Who is he?" asked the hedgehog.

"Some sort of alley cat. A low, cunning villain what's the brains behind it all. Now what do they call him? . . . Mangy . . . no, that's not it . . . what's the fellow's drat-

8

ted name?" Dink scratched his head in his slow way. He blinked sleepily with the effort of thinking before rubbing his chin to jog his memory. But it was Quill who remembered for him.

"Could it be . . . could it be Mungo Brown?" asked Quill shakily.

Dink's face rarely registered surprise, but when it did, it was a slow process. Like dawn breaking across a hillside in winter or a spring tide just on the turn; surprise started somewhere at chest level before hauling itself onto his face. It climbed into his eyes which opened wide, then closed, then opened wider. "That's it!" he drawled. "You got it. But how did *you* know?"

"He was the rogue who started all the trouble in the Great Beyond. He was set free about three years ago and left the country. No one heard of him since . . . till now!" said Quill. "And to think of it, here in our own Domusland!"

"He's called himself Chairman of the Shire Moot in Black Wood. An' it's him what's grabbed our Derry's land," said Dink grimly.

Had he but known it, the Wastelanders had grabbed more than Derry's land. They'd nabbed Derry himself! From what Dink went on to tell Quill, it seemed things had changed alarmingly during the time Quill had been away in the summer. He realised just how much he was out of touch; so much so, he resolved to visit Black Wood the next day, to find out for himself just what was happening.

Chapter 2

Snow had fallen steadily through the night. Indeed, it had been such a heavy fall that when Quill went to see what the weather was like before bidding Dink goodnight, he had been taken by surprise and insisted that Dink stay the night. Of course, Dink had said he could find his way home all right, but it was only token resistance. All decent Meadowfolk had spare rooms, or at the very least, spare beds and bunks for guests caught by bad weather. Even when the weather was tolerably good and guests had come from a distance, it was not unusual for them to stay the night if the company and food were going splendidly. Sociable evenings were never disrupted by such unhallowed practices as "going home." One never went home anyhow from a good party. One was already "at home" and simply took it to bed in the early hours of the morning. "Going home" began after a lie-in and a late breakfast, when conversation on all topics was just about exhausted.

So when Quill got up the next morning, Dink was still fast asleep in the spare room at the top of Oak Tree. The ashes of the fire were glowing, half-awake like Quill, who pottered about in his down-at-heel slippers and red dressing gown. He threw a handful of kindling into the grate and pushed some life into it with the bellows. Once flames were dancing up the chimney, he was able to leave them to their own devices, springing and leaping from one log to another to see who could bound furthest up the chim-ney. Then he went into the kitchen to see about breakfast.

Now both dorfolk and hedgehogfolk are very partial to porridge, and Quill was an expert porridge-maker. He cooked it just right—not too thick and lumpy; and not too thin and gruelly. It was just right.

"Beautiful!" he murmured to himself, as he took a fin-gerful of delicious porridge off the wooden thimble he'd been stirring it with. "It should be exactly done by the time that old snorer gets down here." He glanced at the cuckoo clock on the wall. As if acknowledging his look, the little bird inside popped out and gave ten fluty cuck-oos before locking itself up for another hour. Quill took out his pocket watch, given him years before by his Uncle Ben. He wound it up, muttering, "Losing again. It's the snow. Always gets behind this weather. Won't make it up again till spring."

Putting his watch back, he opened the door to the stair-case inside the hollow of the oak. "Dink!" he shouted. "Time to get up! Your porridge is ready!"

A muffled reply, a dreamy sort of reply, floated down from two storeys up, followed by a thud and a long, Dorry yawn which came all the way down into the kitchen. There it was seized by the wind, carried up the flue into the outside world, and taken to the place where all good yawns end their days. A minute or two later Dink came down in a borrowed dressing gown, scratching his head and trying vainly to muffle another yawn.

"It's stopped snowing," said Dink, rubbing a pane of glass and peering out.

"Should be able to reach your place without too much trouble," commented Quill, doling out a healthy help-ing of porridge into Dink's bowl. "Help yourself to syrup, Dink."

11

The dormouse needed no second bidding. He dipped his spoon into the jar and pulled out a plug of syrup, twisting it neatly to cut off its tail. Then he let it slide from his spoon in a delicious, glistening waterfall which curled into a heap momentarily before spreading in a yellow lake across the top of his porridge. When the syrup had thinned to a trickle, he wrote his name "Dink," and that hung legibly a second before blurring into the porridge. The ritual complete, he stirred his bowl and then began eating.

"Never tasted better porridge than yours, Quill," he said, dipping his spoon again deeply. "Not even my grannie could beat this—and she prided herself at porridge-making. You've a touch all your own."

Quill mumbled something about it being a hedgehog speciality, then he tucked into his own bowl. He stood near the window looking out, for hedgehogs always eat their porridge standing, like every good porridger. Then the two porridged away in silence till their bowls were quite empty, and having scraped them clean, they wiped their mouths with the linen napkins and sat back to sip tea.

"I've been thinking," said Quill at length. "In fact, I thunk a great deal after we'd turned in last night, and it seems to me a visit ought to be paid on Mungo Brown . . . or at least on what he's up to in Black Wood."

"I been thinking similar," offered Dink.

"And I've always thought two opinions are better than one," commented Quill. "Especially if they agree."

"An' they're safer," added Dink.

"*Much* safer," Quill agreed. "Never know what you may meet en route."

"Or who," said Dink.

"Or whom," Quill echoed, rather more grammatically. "That dratted alley cat has a knack of turning up just at the wrong time—and more often than the proverbial bad penny. If there's a dirty deed in the offing, then that cat will be behind it."

12

Dink coughed and looked puzzled, then asked, "What's an offing?" Dink's schooling was not of the best, yet he often finished with right answers when more educated folk never got them at all.

"An offing?" said Quill, who himself looked puzzled now. "An offing is—er—I suppose the opposite of an onning."

"Oh," said Dink, attempting to look more enlightened; but after Quill had cast a hurried glance in his direction, he decided more explanation was needed.

"And an onning is—er—what's on now, er—what's happening at present. So, an offing is what's just off the boil, so to speak. What's still to come. It hasn't happened yet."

"Thank you," said the dormouse, looking mightily relieved. "I'm much obliged."

Quill went on, "Now it's my belief there's a dirty deed in the offing in that alley cat's head. I propose we go over to your place and pick up some things for you, once I've packed for the trip to Black Wood. We may be there a while, and the quicker we get there, the quicker we can act to stop Mungo Brown's offing turning into an onning."

"Good idea," said Dink, "and while you pack, I'll wash up." Which was just what they did.

The hedgehog was a neat fellow and knew precisely where things were which he needed for his travels. After all, he was quite used to travelling now, so it wasn't long before he was back with his rucksack packed and his tartan hold-all full to the zip. He was dressed in his travelling gear: quilted anorak, waterproof leggings, thick mitts, and he carried the cudgel he'd used so effectively the last time the Wastelanders had crossed his path.

"Aar!" said Dink, quite impressed by the sudden transformation from dressing gown to travelling gear. "You have been sharp. Don't know as how I could get myself rigged like that if I packed all morning!"

"Then the sooner we'd get to your place, the better. Come on, Dink," said Quill, "get yourself dressed and we'll be off."

While Dink was upstairs, Quill finished tidying his little living room and kitchen. He thought he might be away for a few days, but had he known just how long he was to be away, he'd have done more than tidy up, he'd have swathed the place in dust covers! It was a stroke of good fortune, too, that he left a note for Mrs. Blossom, a distant cousin on his mother's side who came and did for him twice a week. He scribbled her a quick note, then stuck it behind the tea caddy in the kitchen. "Dear Mrs. Blossom," he began, "I've gone to Black Wood to Dink Dormouse's cousin to see what's happening there. I've heard there's something strange going on. Mungo Brown seems to be behind it all. Please tell old Kraken the raven and say *on no account* must he have any dealings with any rats who come into the Meadow Shire wanting to buy land. I remain, your affectionate cousin, Quill." He paused a moment after writing his letter then went on, "P.S. Cancel the milk. Dink Dormouse is going with me."

By the time he'd written it, Dink was ready, so making sure the fire was all right and the door well latched, the two animals set off for Dormouse Cottage in the Dingle.

The snow was deep, and it took them the best part of an hour to reach Dink's cottage. They met no one on the way for, although it had stopped snowing, the wind had whipped up the loose snow into drifts which made the going tough. They spoke little. They needed all their breath to tackle the drifts they ploughed through, so they arrived at the cottage in silence. But imagine their surprise when they turned the corner of the copse leading to Dink's path to see two magpies; one knocking loudly on Dink's door, the other peering rudely through his living room window.

14

Magpies at Dink's cottage

Quill quickly pulled Dink behind the trees out of sight, for the dormouse had stopped in his tracks with his mouth wide open. "Wait!" he said softly. "Let's see what those two are up to. You don't get magpiefolk in the Dingle at this time of year."

"Well, I never!" was all Dink could muster, once he'd shut his mouth, which was getting distinctively cold inside. "Looking through my window! I never known such tricks! They oughter be ashamed!"

But it wasn't long before it became quite clear what the pair were up to. The bird looking through the window was joined by the other. Quill and Dink kept to the shadow of the trees and moved steadily closer, their approach muffled by the snow and screened by the large laurel hedge running up to Dink's cottage. Soon, they were so close to the magpies, they could have touched them—which in due course they did.

"Don't seem to be anyone at 'ome, matey," one magpie was saying. "Not a peep from inside."

"Nah, not a peep," echoed the other.

"So?" said the first.

"So," continued the second, "I proposes we lets ourselves in to 'ave a look-see and find that which Chairman Mungo 'as sent us for."

"Exactly my sentiments, Mick," said the first, with a wink. "One bad deed deserves another and one bad cat deserves his day . . . 'specially if it brings us bread." ('Bread,' so I'm told, is the word used in some circles for money; nothing to do with food.) The magpies thought this was a huge joke and cackled coarsely as magpies always do.

One of the birds was fat and large; and one was thin and small, much younger than his partner, too. Clearly an apprentice burglar, for the older, fatter bird had much craft and guile. He had a large watch chain strung brassily across a broad expanse of tummy, like many fat folk in Wasteland. It was he who had been knocking so loudly

16

on the door. They called him Mack the Fat in the profession he followed, and his partner Mick the Thin. Mack, after another squint through the window, pulled out a crowbar from inside his pocket and with a neat flick of his wrist and the minimum of fuss, had the window open. He was a superb burglar. Of that there was no doubt at all.

"Nah then, young fellow," he croaked hoarsely at his accomplice, "in yer goes, an' let me in through the door as soon as poss. I ain't as agile as I once was—not in me legs anyhow, though me headpiece still ticks over." He gave another laugh, then cupped his hands to help the younger burglar in through the window.

"All clear," came back the young one's voice from inside Dink's dining room. "I'll go and let you in now."

The little magpie disappeared, but great was his surprise when he opened the door to let his friend in, for . . . but I'll tell you what happened in a moment. Let's go back to Mack the Fat standing outside the window. He took off his bowler hat to mop his brow after his recent exertion, but he never put it back! Not for some time. Barely had Mick the Thin gone, when a hand holding a cudgel appeared out of the laurel hedge behind him and rapped the fat magpie firmly on the noodle. He went down without a cackle, wondering vaguely as he fell where all the stars had suddenly come from in the middle of the day, before all went black.

Quill hurried to the door with Dink at his elbow. "That ought to keep the fat one quiet for a while," he said grimly, as he and Dink stood side by side waiting for the door to open. They could hear the young magpie singing to himself as he came towards the door. He was singing a popular burglar's song and had just reached the refrain:

"A burglar's lot is happy, is happy, is happy,
A burglar's lot is happy when there's no one in to
  see . . ."

At this point the door opened. It would be impossible to describe the look of surprise which came onto the magpie's face. Astonishment is not the word. His mouth fell open, and he looked at Quill and Dink as if he'd seen ghosts. But he quickly realised there was something rather more substantial before him and began to back down the corridor.

"Aren't you going to invite me in?" said Dink. "After all, it's my house!"

Quill shut the door behind him with the tip of his cudgel. Escape was impossible. The magpie gulped again, louder and more sorrowfully. Beads of sweat appeared on his brow, and he wrung his hands in despair.

"All right, guys both," he said. "It's a fair cop." Then Quill prodded him on the chest with his cudgel, forcing him back into the room by whose window he'd entered.

"Be kind enough to take a seat," he said, pointing to a chair and touching the bird lightly on the shoulder with his stick. The bird sat down staring at the cudgel till it began to fascinate him. He couldn't take his eyes off it as Quill moved it over, by, round, and about the quaking burglar without actually touching him. When Quill had finished admonishing the bird, he left the cudgel standing in a corner like some still, silent guard dog, then he said to Dink, "Keep an eye on this chap while I go and welcome his partner indoors."

Dink glared at the young magpie half-frightening him to death. The terrified bird almost strained his eyes keeping one of them on the cudgel and the other on Dink. "Oh-oh, my young friend," began Dink. "You're going to answer a question or two when Mr. Quill returns. An' don't go a-trying any tricks or giving him wrong answers. There's no telling what he'll do now he's roused. He's a prickly customer at the best of times!"

"N . . . n . . . no, sir. Of course not, guv . . . anything you says, sir," stammered the magpie.

18

So afraid, so terrified of what Quill might do to him was Mick the Thin that his beak chattered in his head till Dink began to feel sorry for him. A sad, young thing he looked as he sat on the edge of his chair, trembling from top to toe, his head bowed and his little bowler hat turning round and round between his hands.

"You been here long?" Dink asked him at length.

"We . . . we got here only a minute or two before your honours," said the other, and then he blurted out, "Please, sir, I didn't mean it. I didn't mean to break into your house. I was put up to it . . . we was both put up to it by Chairman Mungo Brown. He said he was going to send us to Wasteland as slaves with all the others if we didn't do as he said."

Dink vaguely wondered what the magpie was talking about when he mentioned "slaves," but Dink thought no more about it. Two large tears had appeared in the magpie's eyes. They grew and grew till they could grow no more. Slowly they spilled over, ran down his cheek, along his beak, and plopped heavily into his hat. Dink shifted uneasily. He was a very soft-hearted dormouse and didn't really know what to say except, "Blow your nose . . . an' stop that sniffling!"

"I ain't got a 'ankie!" blubbed the other.

"Then . . . then borrow mine," said Dink, fishing out a large handkerchief from his pocket.

Mick the Thin took it and blew his nose loudly. Then passed the hankie back.

"You'd better hang onto it. You're going to need it again when Mr. Quill returns. He's in a very bad mood, I can tell you!" said Dink.

And hang onto it the magpie did. He put his bowler hat on the table and sobbed unashamedly into Dink's hankie till Quill reentered with Mack the Fat. The older magpie now looked very deflated. Gone was all the bland assurance. Gone was his quipping. Gone, it seemed, were his senses, for he was brought in looking very dazed and distant. A large lump on his bonce was making an impressive entrance into the world. His two eyes rolled wildly as he tried to count the galaxy of stars swirling before them. He had a headache, and he distinctly heard the twittering of swallows, though the swallows had gone months before—and Mack was beginning to wish he'd gone with them.

Gradually the twittering faded, the stars went back into orbit, and his two eyes stopped rolling. They became fixed on Quill and he knew the game was up. Mack put his head in his wings. His watch chain sagged several inches. He'd been copped!

Chapter 3

I t didn't take Quill long to get from the magpies what he wanted to know. A few threats, a little waving of his cudgel, a little cajolery, and he knew all he wanted—and more. Apparently, Mack the Fat and Mick the Thin had been sent to steal Derry Dormouse's deeds to his house and farm. He'd given them to Dink for safekeeping the last time they'd met. Like all bullies, the Wastelanders wanted to give their evil doings a pretence of rightness. Like many people in power, they wanted everything to look as if it were legal, when, in fact, it wasn't; so they'd forced Derry to sign a document selling them his land—at a very low price—but they needed documents to make it *look* right. However, where Derry was now, not even the magpies knew. They suspected he'd been taken back to Wasteland and locked up there. They spoke of mysterious disappearances in the middle of the night, when the Black Jackets whipped folk from their homes, folk never seen again. That was why, Mack explained, they had gone over to the Wasteland side—to preserve their own cowardly skins.

"But how did you know our Derry had given me the deeds?" asked Dink.

"They put the finger on 'im I 'spect," growled Mack. "They ain't like our coppers. Them Black Jackets give you the old one-two before they ask you questions."

Even Quill looked puzzled at this, while Dink simply stared blankly. He'd barely understood a word. The magpie began to explain.

"You see, guvs both, when these Wastelanders wants something bad, they act bad to get it. They have ways of making you talk I wouldn't begin to tell you about, and there ain't one of 'em what's pleasant. You'd tell 'em anything to stop 'em. An' when they've got what they want, they carts you off to their factories to work for nothing or they locks you up in gaol. They fingered us early on when we was . . . well, when we was looking over one of their joints . . . nabbed us as soon as we set foot inside . . . just like you, guv . . . 'cept you ain't fingering us like them."

"Why did they let you go free then?" asked Quill.

"Because we're useful to 'em, me an' Mick. We're professionals—first- and second-class burglars with certificates to prove it. They don't have burglars like us in Wasteland. They don't have our . . . our finesse, guv. But we're done for this time, ain't we? I mean, if we don't go back with those deeds we'll be sent down with the rest, slaving in some blooming Wasteland factory." Mack sank back quite deflated, almost on the point of needing Mick's handkerchief, but that young bird was still mopping up his own downpour.

"So that's their game, is it?" said Quill. "They're trying to do here what they failed to do in the Great Beyond. Mungo Brown is trying to take over Domusland."

"What can we do?" asked Dink.

Quill said nothing for a moment but looked thoughtfully at the magpie. Mack never could look anyone in the eye and stared at the ceiling. Mick blew loudly into Dink's hankie. After a while Mack could stand the tension no longer and said hoarsely, "If there's anything we can do, guv, I mean if you wants to use our hexpert services, so to speak, we'll be only too glad to help. You made a fair

22

cop an' I don't see as we can go back to them Wastelanders
now. They didn't really appreciate us anyway . . . sending us after deeds . . . not our line at all. Nah if they'd
wanted antique silver . . ." And Mack's eyes lit up most
professionally as he said this.

"I'll tell you what I'll do," said Quill at length. "If you'll
agree to help us, we'll say no more about this disgraceful
episode of breaking and entering, for that's what it is,
finesse or no finesse. If you'll help us we'll forget all about
it . . . otherwise, you know as well as I do, you're in for a
long spell in the Meadowland cop-shop."

"We'll help!" chorused the magpies.

"Then you'll tell us all you know about what Mungo
Brown is up to, where he's living in Domusland, what's
happened to the folk who have disappeared and what else
is going on in the Black Wood Shire," said Quill.

The magpies told him all they knew. Quill learned a
great deal from them; a great deal, indeed. Things were
far worse than he expected, for Mungo was planning new
factories not only in Black Wood but for all Domusland,
including Hedgehog Meadow. Quill heard about multi-
national companies housed in multi-purpose complexes—
though he had only a vague idea of what these terms
meant. Mack told him of multi-storey blocks going up
in Wasteland containing offices which housed a multi-
plicity of rats all engaged in duplicity of one sort or
another in the world of multi-business.

"Wasteland Enterprises Inc." the new consortium was
called, led by Chairman Mungo Brown. It had subsidiary
companies like "Mungo Brown Ltd." or "Chat et Rat
Associes S.A.A." or "Wuste G.M.B.H."—all multi-fronts
for Mungo's multifarious deeds. Choose your own language, it was all the same. Mungo's glib tricks in whatever tongue added up to getting, grabbing, and gratifying
his own unsatisfied urge for power. If anyone got in his
way, that was too bad. He simply took them over, buying

23

them out as cheaply as possible. If that did not work, they disappeared through the Tunnel to Wasteland.

Quill realised they had to tread carefully. Somehow they had to see what Mungo was up to without getting caught. If they could spy out the land before going to the Great Beyonders, it would be most helpful, but how? He had an idea.

"You said just now that Mungo issues identity cards to all his workers, those he can trust. Have you got one?" Quill asked the birds.

Mick the Thin drew out a greasy card from his pocket. It read: "This is to certify that Mick the Thin, B.A., is authorised to burglarise on instructions from the head of police only. Please admit to such premises as warranted. Signed Mungo Brown. President Wasteland Enterprises Inc., Ratburg New Town, Mungoville, Wasteland, MB1."

Quill looked surprised. "B.A.," he said. "I didn't know you'd been to college and got a Bachelor of Arts!"

"The B.A. means burglar apprentice. That's all," said Mick.

Mack the Fat's card was similar, except he had "M.B." on his card, master burglar. Quill returned their cards and commented, "We also shall have to get fixed up with I.D. cards or we shall never get into Wasteland." But there he was quite wrong. He and Dink were to arrive in Wasteland, without I.D. cards, far quicker than they thought!

Mack touched his bowler hat respectfully, looking most turned-over-a-new-leafish. "If you please, guv," he began, "me an' my assistant 'ere could help you gents get into Wasteland by a devious route, so to speak." He ended by giving Quill and Dink a wink.

"How?" asked Quill.

"By going under the Mystery Marshes," said Mack. "The Wastelanders have built a Tunnel from their side of the marshes to Domusland."

"Never!" Quill exclaimed.

"True, guv. Sure as my name's Mack the Fat. An' me an' Mick will take you two gents there this very afternoon, if you'll be so good as to come."

There was little option if the animals were to make it to Black Wood that day but to trust the magpies—and trust them they did, to their great surprise. The Tunnel was nearer—and far larger—than they'd ever supposed. They found this out after they'd been trudging behind Mack and Mick for two hours. There was still some distance to go before Black Wood was reached, when they halted at an outcrop of rock on the crest of a ridge. Thankfully the four animals huddled behind it to get out of the biting wind. They were all tired, too, and glad of a break.

"Phew!" said Mack. "It ain't half hard going in this snow. It's got deeper since this morning, ain't it, Mick?"

His partner nodded. Though he'd followed Mack's footsteps all the way from Dink's cottage and benefited enormously from fat Mack, who pushed his way through the snow like a roly-poly snowplough, Mick was cold and miserable. He thrust his wings under his wingpits and stamped his feet to bring some life back to them.

Dink looked across the landscape from the shelter of the rocks. "We're well off the track to Black Wood," he commented. "Folk rarely come up this way, 'cept the moorsfolk. There ain't a road near here for miles."

"This isn't a trick, is it?" asked Quill suspiciously.

"Guv, guv!" pleaded Mack, looking very hurt. "We give our word, didn't we? We're pledged, me an' Mick, to help you—an' a burglar never goes back on his word; leastways, not certificated burglars like us."

"Well, we'll see," Quill mumbled.

"You'll see, indeed, guvs both. You're a-going to see something now what your eyes ain't never seen before. Now what do you make of that?" he asked confidently, pointing to a large boulder.

"A rock. That's all," Quill replied, a little mystified.

25

*Magpies, Quill, and Dink at the
entrance to the shaft*

"But that ain't all," continued the other triumphantly. "Now if you two gents just come along o' me, I'll show you something what'll make your two eyes open very wide."

The magpie walked towards the boulder. Round its base were many little prints—rat-prints! They were somewhat blurred by the snow, but there they were none the less. All of them ended just in front of the massive boulder.

"What's going on here?" asked Quill, pointing to the prints.

"Them's rats!" Dink exclaimed.

"Right first time, guv," said Mack rather patronisingly. "Them's rats right enough—Wasteland rats!"

"But . . . but where did they come from? What are they doing here?" asked the hedgehog.

Mack the Fat did not answer. He walked round the boulder, slowly felt along part of it, then pulled back a small, hidden panel which lay flush with the surface. Inside was a button. He pressed it, and slowly, very slowly, the huge stone began to swing back to reveal a large, black hole— the entrance to a shaft leading into the Tunnel! As the rock swung open, so did Quill and Dink's mouths. They both gasped, and Mack's triumph was complete.

"What did I tell you, gents both? Now do you believe me?" said Mack.

"It's incredible!" said Quill at length. "How did it get here?"

"Hunderground hunderhandedness, guv," aspirated Mack. "I'll explain all later, but now I think we ought to step inside. Something tells me there's a gang of rats around here, an' we don't want to be nabbed when they come back. I've been nabbed enough for one day," he added ruefully.

Quill nodded and followed the birds into the blackness. Once inside, the magpie touched another button and a great wall of rock clanged fast behind them. Mack picked up a storm lamp just inside and lit it. As it flickered to life, it threw long, distorted shadows of the four animals on the walls. Their voices also sounded eerie, echoing mournfully down the shaft into the blackness in front, and instinctively they huddled more closely together.

"This shaft leads into the Tunnel what goes direct to Wasteland right under the marshes. Mungo brings all his supplies through it—an' takes back the Domuslanders he's nabbed over here as slave labour. His police is every-where now. That'll be some of 'em whose prints we saw outside. They're scouting everywhere in Domusland," said Mack, as they trudged carefully down the shaft.

It was dark and wet. Damp ploppings came from all about them. In front, a long way ahead, was a muffled noise; as if from huge machines worked by many hands. Quill marvelled how Mungo Brown had achieved all this so secretly and so fast. But that is the way of evil genius, isn't it? The good things in life take longer to develop and are done in the open.

They'd been going about twenty minutes towards the noise in front which grew louder and louder. Clearly work was progressing at a furious rate. The sound of drills and diggers became clearer. They heard the noise of clanging and banging as trucks were rolled up and down. Rubble was being shovelled and cleared—and over it all, high-pitched rat voices could be heard cursing and shouting orders. Then other sounds reached their ears, too, from behind! The quartet stopped and listened, listened so hard they dare scarcely breathe.

Sure enough there came the steady crunch of feet marching behind.

"It's them police what's come back!" whispered Mack.

"Oh, me! Oh, my!" gulped Mick, "What we goin' to do? If they catch us, Mack, they'll . . ." He left his sentence unfinished. The thought of what might happen to them was too horrible for the young magpie to contemplate. The light in Mack's hand started shaking as he, too, considered what might happen.

"Let's move on," he croaked. "We can't go back."

They didn't need a second bidding and scuttled blindly down the shaft. Alas, their speed was their undoing because a few hundred yards further on, the shaft turned a corner. So intent were they listening to the police behind, they took no account of anything in front, and turning the corner they ran into a Wasteland guard. None of them could stop. The guard went flying as the fat magpie bumped into him. Quill tripped over Mick, who'd gone headlong over his partner. Dink, short-sighted as ever, never really knew what happened. All he saw one moment was Quill hurtling into space, and the next he was looking through his own two feet at the roof above. A cry rang up the shaft and more lights appeared. The marching behind grew faster, and within seconds they were all prisoners of the Wasteland rats!

Chapter 4

I t took Quill some time to work out just how he came to be sitting in a very cold prison cell with handcuffs on his wrists and heavy chains around his ankle. Opposite him was Dink similarly bound, while at the further end of the cell two very dejected magpies moaned and shivered all the time. They shivered so much their chains shook and rattled like a spectre with a bad cold.

"What happened?" asked Quill, feeling the bump on his head.

"We was jumped," moaned Mack, feeling his head, which now, like the Bactrian camel, was the proud possessor of two bumps. "Then we was thumped! You shouldn't have put up such a fight, guv. They'd have taken us quietly if you'd left 'em alone."

Slowly it all came back to Quill, the splendid, if brief, fight they had put up in the Tunnel.

"You did for two of 'em, Quill," said Dink. "I saw two of them rats go down, before you was hit on the head."

Quill felt bad, but the magpies looked worse. The police rats had given them a pretty rough time for they hated them on two counts: first, because they were burglars, and second, because they were Domuslanders, and there was little love lost between those folk. The birds' coats were torn, their hats dented, and their feathers quite out of ruffle. Nevertheless, it proved one thing to Quill. The magpies had kept their word. There was no doubt whose side they were on now. Indeed, there was no doubt at all which side they were all on. They were all on the wrong side of a firmly locked door.

"What we goin' to do, guv?" asked Mack through a jangle of chains.

"First of all," said Quill, whose headache grew worse with every jangle, "you and Mick are going to sit still and stop rattling those wretched chains! We must all of us think—a long, hard think about what to do next."

So they sat in silence and thunk. They had been thinking only a short while, when an evil chuckle came through the door. It came from the peep-hole which had been opened to allow a particularly evil eye to peep in.

The chuckle was followed by an over-oiled voice which purred, "I trust you have thought up something worthwhile—not concerned with escape. Nothing can save you now. You have my word on that!"

Quill glanced up, shading his eyes from the glare of the light. He peered hard at the door a moment, then gasped, "Mungo Brown!" as the cell door opened and a cat stepped inside.

"Right first time," came the cool reply—and Mungo it was; fatter, much fatter, and sleeker, dressed in a costly pinstripe suit with a heavy, gold watch chain hung across a disgustingly heavy paunch. It was Mungo all right with the same hard, greedy eyes and cruel mouth. "This is a surprise, Quill Hedgehog. I really never expected to meet up with you quite so soon, though it was inevitable sooner or later. I was rather hoping it might have been later, on more fruitful grounds. You might have made a pile of money if you'd stacked your cards right and played the game my way. But as it is you've saved me much inconvenience and, what's better, a great deal of expense. I shall now be able to acquire Hedgehog Meadow without spend-

31

ing one Mungo mark—and having your patch of ground will go a long way to help me get control of all Domusland. It will keep my capital intact and give me a base to work from right in the heart of your country. The Meadow is just right for development. I can see it now . . . an estate of luxurious executive houses built right across it will make me a handsome packet. Let me see . . . let me see . . ." And here the scoundrel actually started counting on his fingers doing a quick bit of mental arithmetic. "Yes, Hedgehog Meadow suitably developed will net me a cool two million Mungo marks profit. Think of that!" And as Mungo himself thought of it, his eyes narrowed with greedy delight. "Two million sheer profit! You cost me a pretty packet after that Hilltop Inn fiasco—and I've never forgotten that."

The cat was referring to an episode during the struggle ousting the Wastelanders from the Great Beyond, when Quill had sabotaged a cartload of weapons on its way to Mungo's stronghold. Its loss had led to Mungo's defeat and the rats' expulsion from that country.

"No, I've never forgotten that—and never forgiven you. I've sworn revenge on you and all those Great Beyonders a thousand times. And now I have you in my power." He plugged a fat cigar into his mouth, and the jewels on his fat fingers flashed brightly.

"You'll never get away with it," said Quill grimly.

"Who's to stop me, pray?" asked the cat quite coolly, knocking off the ash from his cigar. "Who's to stop me doing just what I want now in Domusland?"

Quill was about to make an angry reply, but he could see that losing his temper would get him nowhere. He glared silently at the smug, feline face as Mungo continued, "You're going to have a long holiday, a long holiday in Wasteland. I'm sending you back through the Tunnel to join the other Domuslanders we have there. We've made quite a pleasant holiday camp for you all, so do enjoy yourself."

He gave another evil laugh, then turned round and strolled out. A guard closed the door behind him and silence, soggy, sad silence descended on the cell again. But they were not left alone for long. The sound of tramping feet was heard in the corridor and a posse of rats came in.

"Come on, you lot!" squeaked their leader. "You're in for a long haul today!"

They were released from the wall, but their legs and wrists remained secured. The magpies were marched out, then Dink and Quill. They were taken first to Black Wood, to Mungo's huge bungalow which was screened by trees and surrounded by a high electric fence. Black Jackets were everywhere, huge, ugly-looking rats who wore high-peaked hats with the death's head emblem on. They carried pistols and truncheons, which they were always keen to use. Mungo never went anywhere without his Black Jacket guards who were supervised by a colonel, a major, and a captain, trusty aides who never left his side—nor ceased to flatter him.

The bungalow was built in extensive grounds on the edge of the Lyth. It was a much larger version of the grandest executive-style houses he hoped to build in Hedgehog Meadow. It was brash and vulgar, like Mungo. Like him, it had windows you could look out of but not into. They were dark and reflected with a metallic sheen what was outside. They gave not the slightest hint of what might lay inside—except darker deeds. The lawns about the place looked too green, too neatly kept. They had none of the mongrelly mixture of clover and moss laced with a rich variety of weeds like daisies and dandelions that my lawn has. There was also a selection of plastic gnomes looking at plastic fish which plastic storks never caught, though they stared endlessly into the depths of plastic pools. Only the ice capping the water was real and felt most out of place.

Mungo had put on a thick, fur coat to greet his guests. They shivered in the drab prison uniforms they'd been given. Behind them the snow threw into relief the black scars which bulldozers had ripped across the land. There was a messy, muddy wound where Spring Coppice had been. It had congealed temporarily in the frost and snow but would begin to bleed when the warmer weather arrived and the bulldozers could start their dreadful carnage again. Right across the vista the sight was repeated in black patches, almost to the horizon. Whole woods had gone, and only the grubbed-up roots of their trees remained clutching helpless at the sky. At intervals were clusters of aluminium caravans, mobile homes in which the rat workers slept. There was also a hard-lined row of prefabricated barracks, protected by rolls of barbed-wire and here the police rats and Black Jackets lived.

Guarded by his aides, Mungo strolled casually along his escarpment, well wrapped up and smoking a fat cigar. His three yes-men were yessing well and strolled in step with their master, smiling and fawning all the time. Mungo rolled rather than walked. He had become an exceedingly fat alley cat to be sure and looked like a huge, fur ball as he waddled along the path. Guarded by soldiers, his four prisoners were forced to follow dismally, shivering with cold and their irons chafing their skin.

"You see, my good friend Quill, and . . . what's your colleague's name?" purred Mungo.

"Dink Dormouse, sir," oiled the rat captain, always anxious to keep in with the cat.

"He's the cousin of Derry Dormouse, the fellow we had all the trouble with, sir," interrupted the major, not to be outdone.

"The one I removed to Wasteland and trained as a waiter. He's back here now . . . serving on the land he once owned. I thought that might please you, sir," beamed the colonel, asserting his authority over the two others.

34

"Good chappies," said Mungo, smiling benevolently on his three henchmen. "You are all such good chappies!" And the colonel and the major and the captain exchanged huge winks with each other behind Mungo's back, for they liked to keep their boss happy. He always gave them presents when he was in a good mood. "Excellent," he purred again, and took a huge, self-satisfied puff at his cigar. Then he continued, "You see, in the not too distant future I shall build new factories, new towns, new cities here—all to create new wealth."

The cat oozed greed, which flavoured his entire house. He closed his eyes in bliss as the prospect of more wealth rose before him. A slow, self-congratulatory smile inched his fat cheeks further up his collar, and when he opened his eyes again, it would not have surprised anyone looking at him to see moneybags reflecting in them. "Oh, yes," he drawled, "I shall bring prosperity to these parts such as it's never dreamed of. I shall bring competence, efficiency, riches . . ."

"Nonsense!" yelled Quill, quite unable to contain his anger any more. "Nonsense! You'll bring dirt and squalor, violence and terror—just as you did in the Great Beyond. You and those like you are the only ones who benefit from your kind of change. Everyone else becomes your slaves!"

The smile slid off the cat's face dropping into his furcoat. He blew out a cloud of smoke irritably and glared at Quill. The captain, who was nearest, dug him spitefully in the ribs with his cane and told him to shut up. Everyone suffered when Mungo was displeased. "You'll be sorry for this!" hissed the major. "Bread and water for you when you're back inside!" stormed the colonel. But Mungo said nothing. He simply looked coldly in the hedgehog's direction and ordered him to be taken to Wasteland along with the others. His tail twitched just the tiniest bit to show he was angry; then he strolled back to his warm bungalow.

The quartet of prisoners was driven down the escarpment to the Tunnel. By the time they arrived, they were shivering bitterly. Mick had fallen twice on the way down and had been kicked to his feet by their guards. Their ankles were bleeding from their chains, and they were chilled to the bone.

They were glad to reach the Tunnel for it was warm, and they were pushed onto a long bench where other Domuslanders were seated, slaves of the Wastelanders and workers in the Tunnel. A bell rang and a rat supervisor barked an order. The prisoners laying rail-tracks stopped working and stepped back. A rumbling noise drew closer from the blackness beyond. A minute later, warning lights began to flash on the overhead signals. Then two huge eyes appeared down the Tunnel and a sleek engine drew up pulling a luxury coach. It hooted its horns as it came alongside, and Quill could see fat Wastelanders, well wrapped up against the cold, start to leave.

From where he was, he had a good view of everything. The interior was all padded and tasselled richly. Fine, velvet hangings decorated the windows and walls, and the whole coach reeked of cigar smoke and fine living. A waiter was busy clearing the remains of a sumptuous meal, as outside a guard of honour came smartly to attention before escorting an official party to Mungo's house.

"Who are they?" Quill asked a fellow prisoner.

"They're the new Wasteland Control Commission what's taken over from the old Black Wood Moot. Them with the briefcases and dark specs are directors of the Black Wood Development Corporation. Mungo Brown's their boss," was the reply.

A shrill voice stopped further conversation. "Get along, you idle peasants! You've stood about long enough. Load up these trucks!" A guard cracked a whip and the frightened animals shambled to a line of trucks waiting to be loaded with goods for Wasteland. Once they'd done their task, they themselves were herded into an open truck at the rear of the train. The engine at the front gave a whistle and they were off, shivering again as the cold wind rushed about them. They were on their way under the Mystery Marshes—to Wasteland!

Chapter 5

A week went by. Then another. As the third week began and no Quill appeared, Mrs. Blossom was very worried, indeed. She'd passed on Quill's message to Kraken, as Quill had asked her to do before leaving. It was just as well, for shortly after he'd gone, some minkfolk from Black Wood came to the Meadow, trying to purchase land and houses at the most outrageous prices; threatening folk that if they didn't sell cheaply, they'd jolly well have their land taken from them before long.

It was only when P.C. Brock Badger told them to clear off and stop pestering that they went; not, I might add, without veiled threats to that stalwart of the law which resulted in their names going in his book. They cared not a jot, though, and one of them even jeered at the constable before he left—a thing unheard of before in the Meadow.

The Meadowfolk were puzzled, no one more than Mick Mole, who lived right on the edge of the Meadow Shire next to Black Wood Shire. He reported strange, underground noises rumbling beneath his home. Cracks had appeared in his kitchen walls and so vigorous had been the rumblings at one stage, the picture of his great-greatgrandfather on his mother's side had fallen and broken the frame. He was happy to report, though, that his greatgreat-grandfather was still intact.

It didn't take Kraken long, wise bird that he was, to put two and two together. Something sinister was going on, and he linked that something with Mungo Brown. A pink-faced Mrs. Blossom appearing out of breath at the raven's door one morning with Quill's note in her hand, her voluminous, polka-dotted dress and red pinafore quite windblown and hair very much out of prickle under her bonnet, convinced him that the two and two he had put together had grown to four and four. Things were getting decidedly grim, and it was time he was off—off to the Great Beyond for help.

So he calmed Mrs. Blossom and told her in no uncertain terms that she was not to let any strangers into Oak Tree, that she was to tell nothing to anyone she didn't know, and that she was to go immediately to the Elders of the Meadow Moot and instruct them, on his behalf, to sell no land to anyone on any account. They were to be vigilant. They were to watch out for rum customers. They were to instruct the Moot Militia to prepare moot pikes and muskets for possible action and they were to . . . but at this point Mrs. Blossom's cup was shaking so dangerously in her saucer that Kraken thought it better to shut up.

"Pikes and muskets!" exclaimed the old widow. "Whatever is the Meadow coming to? There ain't been any fighting in Meadow Shire since I don't know when . . . not since some of them Black Wood varmints came raiding our orchards in my dad's time! That was when P.C. Brock's dad—Sergeant Brock as was—called in help from the next Shire constabulary."

"This is more serious than apple raids," said Kraken, his watery old eyes glinting fiercely. He moved his venerable specs up his beak an inch or two, for they had a habit of slipping down when he spoke. He spent more time peeping over them these days than he did looking through them. "This is a very serious matter if I'm right,

Mrs. Blossom, and the quicker we get help, the better. I'm going to the Great Beyond, to Quill's friends there. They'll know what to do. They've had to deal with this villain, Mungo Brown, before. It wouldn't surprise me in the least if that young adventurer, Quill Hedgehog, hasn't gone and gotten himself into some kind of scrape. The number of times I've told him not to go wandering off so; but he never listens." The raven sighed deeply and wiped his specs. "Don't know where he gets it from. The Quills have always been settled, home-loving folk as long as I've known . . . and that's going back a bit now."

The old bird took Mrs. Blossom's cup from her and ushered her through his door back to the Meadow. Being a wily, old raven he locked his door securely and hid the key in a place so secret I can't even mention it here. He took one final look around, stretched his wings, flapped them stiffly a time or two, then flew off into the sun towards the Great Beyond.

In a short while the Staying Hills were far below him. Their snowy, rounded tops gleamed in the sunlight. The river, too, glinted and wound its way through fields and woods, unrolling like a silver ribbon till it reached Fitzworthy Castle. There it made a gentle loop round that noble edifice before meandering away out of sight to the other side of the land.

The leafless hedgerows etched the fields with black, patchwork borders into all shapes and sizes. Here and there, little knots of sheep clustered round feeding troughs, their breath streaming out in fine vaporous clouds. The air was still and frosty, so frosty you felt it would crack. But far below, their dainty hooves had pricked tiny holes in the mud, freed a while from its icy prison by the sun.

As he drew nearer the castle, Kraken heard the shouts of young folk skating round and round the frozen moat; and as his aged eyes brought the scene into focus, the raven

40

saw Horatio Fitzworthy, Quill's great friend, the aristocratic cat, stoking a brazier on the land side of the moat, roasting spuds and chestnuts which he distributed freely as the skaters came up to him. There was a constant flow of them, replenishing breakfasts they'd skated away long since, or warming frozen fingers and toes at the brazier.

There was an empty stretch of ice near the brazier on which Horatio was placing a new row of potatoes. Most of the skaters had dashed off in a screaming gaggle to join a race which took them round the other side of the castle. Kraken noted that empty expanse of ice, and to this day he doesn't know what possessed him to land on it the way he did. Possibly it was the sight of all those young skaters which injected him with a shot of misplaced energy. Certainly, it was on sheer impulse, a vision of younger, more sprightly days which rushed into his head and made him act the way he did. He came in to land quite recklessly, exactly as he'd done often many, many years before. Even as he touched the ice he regretted it! He lost his balance, skidded, hung precariously one terrible second with one foot braking on the ice as the other clawed frantically somewhere near his beak. His wings thrashed madly at the air as he tried to regain his balance. But no! It was not to be. He toppled over on his back, a spinning heap of untidy feathers landing almost at Horatio's feet. His spectacles hung across his beak and he had to wait a moment till the little twitters in his head had silenced; till the castle, yes, the whole of that noble structure which a moment before had been so solid and immovable, had finished tumbling and somersaulting and gone back into place.

Horatio looked calmly at the dishevelled, squawking bundle which dropped at his feet. He helped the old bird up and dusted him down, putting his specs back into place. "Well, well, well, if it isn't my good friend Kraken," he said quietly, in his old, imperturbable manner. "How nice of you to drop in. Care for a spud?"

The cat took a delicious, roasted potato and placed it on a plate with a pair of wooden tongs. Deftly he sliced it in two. It was done to a "T." The floury interior swelled slightly, opening in two halves like white roses for Horatio to drop a pat of golden butter into, which melted and blent with the spud as soon as it touched it.

"Help yourself to salt, my dear chap." said Horatio, passing the raven a salt-cellar.

Kraken didn't need asking twice. His longish flight had given him an appetite till he was in every sense ravenous. Yet, urgent as his news was, appetites and etiquette come first in the animal world. Their priorities are much better judged than ours. It would have been the severest breach of good manners, not to mention the slight he'd have given his stomach, if Kraken had not accepted the potato and eaten it before telling his news.

"Kraa-aa, delicious!" he croaked, spooning it hungrily into his beak and warming his frozen wing-tips on the hot jacket. That part of his anatomy, that unmentionable part, which had skidded on the ice and had become exceedingly cold in the process, he thawed out at the brazier keeping his tail well up to let as much heat as possible warm him.

"Just the sort of weather for a hot spud, eh?" beamed Horatio, helping himself to another potato before dipping his spoon into the mass of steaming flocculence.

"Couldn't agree more," said Kraken, scooping the last spoonful out of a jacket you could see the brown through, he'd whittled it so clean.

"You'll stay with us a while, of course," continued Horatio. "Anyone from Domusland is always welcome here. We never forget old friends, particularly when they come from Quill Hedgehog's line of country. How is that old wanderer keeping these days?"

Kraken took his cue and said, "It's about Quill I've come. You see, he's disappeared. He left a note almost a fortnight ago saying he was off to Black Wood to look into some funny business there. But that's not unusual in itself. There's some rum folks lives there, I'll tell you."

Horatio paused in the act of putting his spoon to his mouth, "Nothing wrong I hope?" he said.

"A great deal, I fear," the raven replied. "That scoundrel Mungo Brown has appeared on the scene again and, as usual, is making himself a blot on the landscape . . . a blot in every way. He's buying up land or seizing it and building his factories and houses everywhere. Trying to turn our beautiful shires into a slumland as he once tried here."

The soft, gentle light which played around Horatio's eyes hardened at the sound of Mungo's name. The fur stood up on his neck, and he placed his potato back on his plate without eating it.

"I thought we'd seen the last of that blighter," he growled. "When we released him from prison, he promised he'd never meddle with us or with our friends again."

"Promises come cheap with alley cats," was all Kraken said, and the old bird ruffled his feathers irritably.

"So it seems," sighed the cat. "But, dash it all, we couldn't keep him locked up forever."

The raven said nothing for a while, pondering what Horatio had said. "You're right," he murmured at length. "It would be most unanimal to have done that. I suppose his type is a problem we've just got to learn to live with like . . . like rain in the middle of picnics."

"Or wasps in jam," added the cat.

"Or even old age and not being able to land properly any more," said Kraken, smiling sadly.

"Come, come," said Horatio trying to cheer him up. "You weren't *so* bad, you know. A slip on the ice happens to the best of us."

He'd hardly got the words out of his mouth when the first of the skaters came whizzing up the final stretch. There was a whole gaggle of younger Great Beyonders, including Rachel Water-Rat, Frisk Otter, and one of his sisters, Olive, closely followed by Vicky Vole. Brushy Fox was in the lead, but as he approached, his skates caught on something for, whoof! his feet shot from under him and there was the most glorious tangle of brush, skates, scarf, and whiskers all in one, spinning through the air towards them. The fox sprawled headlong and slid up to the brazier exactly as Kraken had done a few moments earlier. The others roared with laughter—Frisk Otter, Leap Hare, Big Bill Badger, Swoop Hawk, Vicky Vole, Rachel Water-Rat, and last of all, Hoot Owl. He came in slowly and staidly, skating with his wings behind him and his muffler gently, ever so gently, floating in the breeze. He was in no hurry at all to reach the finishing line, but coasted in hooting a little owl tune softly to himself in time with his skating.

"Freeze my old whiskers silly!" exclaimed the fox. "What happened?" He brushed the ice off his coat and examined his skates. "Just when I thought I'd got the race buttoned up. Well, hello, my dear fellow!" he continued, noticing Kraken for the first time. "If it ain't my good friend Kraken. How are things in Domusland these days? All well, I trust? And that rascal, young Quill, how's he? We don't see much of him here once autumn has set in. Most unsociable then he is, tell him. We'd all like to see more of him, wouldn't we, chaps?" He turned to the other Great Beyonders who were particular friends of the hedgehog and who thought a great deal of him, for he'd helped free them from the Wastelanders.

"That's exactly what Kraken has come about," explained Horatio. "Things don't look at all well in Domusland— far from it! Now if one or two of you will look after the young folks and make sure they're properly fed, I suggest

44

we adjourn to the castle and listen to what Kraken has to tell us."

Some of the older youngsters took over the potato-roasting while the others trooped over the drawbridge into Fitzworthy Castle. They went to Horatio's study where a huge, log fire crackled in the ancestral fireplace.

It was a magnificent room and had been restored to its former glory after the Wastelanders had been expelled, for they had used the castle as their headquarters. Instead of the arrogant, life-sized, glossy photograph of ex-President Mungo Brown hanging over the fireplace, there was now an old master, a painting of a quiet pastoral scene with a hay wagon and horses crossing a ford; a solitary boy of the Humanfolk lying full-length on his stomach, drinking from a brook. It was an idyllic scene, a little old-fashioned, but it captured exactly the atmosphere of the Great Beyond.

Gone, too, were all those dreadful Wasteland insignia— the ugly lightning flash on red flags under the clenched fist of hate. Instead, the mellow panelling mirrored back its own beauty as the firelight caught it. Along one wall, bookshelves crammed with leather-bound volumes gave the room a relaxed and learned air. There was a large, oak desk nearby, and in the middle of the room a solid table with thick, carved legs. Leather-padded chairs stood ranked along the table like dignified retainers, while above, a glass chandelier winked at everything in sight.

"Sit down, you folk, and make yourselves at home. I don't need to tell you that by now," said Horatio, indicating the chairs. Indeed, he didn't need to tell anyone that at all. You felt at home the instant you entered the place.

The animals seated themselves, Kraken taking the seat next to Horatio, who looked very serious. "My friends," he began. "Kraken has some very disturbing news. Quill has been captured by the Wastelanders!"

A gasp of disbelief ran round the table. "I don't believe it!" exclaimed Rachel Water-Rat.

The unfortunate Magpies, Quill, and Dink being taken to Wasteland

"It's true," croaked the raven. "Too true, alas. He set out for the Black Wood days ago to see what the Wastelanders were up to, and he hasn't been seen since. I have it on the best information that he and Dink Dormouse have been taken to Wasteland. They were seen, manacled as prisoners, by a heron flying overhead from Mereful to Domusland; prisoners of Mungo Brown who's built himself an outsize bungalow on the Lyth just beyond Black Wood—or what's left of it."

"The bounder!" shouted Brushy over the hubbub which followed. "The contemptible bounder! After all that Mungo Brown promised if we'd set him free . . . that he'd never set himself up as boss over anyone again . . . that he'd never go near Wasteland . . . that he'd never . . ."

"He's Chairman Mungo now," interrupted Kraken. "Chairman of one huge company that's busy setting up subsidiaries all over the place with names that have no connection with him. But they're all the same. They pretend to take each other over in some silly game they play. As if they think they're tricking folk. They deceive no one but themselves. But what's more alarming is that Mungo's undermining Domusland in his efforts to take us over."

"What do you mean?" asked Vicky Vole.

And Kraken proceeded to tell them all he'd been able to gather about Mungo Brown and what he was doing in Black Wood Shire. All of which added up to a very bleak outlook indeed for Domusland and its people.

"There's that Tunnel which grows bigger daily," he said. "Branches are being pushed out from it everywhere reaching to all parts of Domusland. It's my belief that when the time's ripe, they'll march an army through it and pop up among us all over the place. They did it here once, and they'll do it to us next time. That's why I've come to you for help."

47

A roar of support came from the Great Beyonders. "Of course, we'll help you!" they shouted. "And what's more, we'll start this very day!" said Frisk Otter, banging his fist on the table. "Right now!"

"How?" came a soft but telling hoot through the noisy enthusiasm.

"What was that?" asked Frisk.

"How?" the owl repeated coolly, blinking through his large spectacles.

"Well . . . er . . . Well, we'll simply march to Wasteland and demand Quill's release. Then we'll drive 'em out. Tell 'em to go. Shut down their Tunnel or whatever they're building . . ." said the otter, rather put out by the owl's dampening question.

"You'll march straight into their gaols and stay there," said Hoot, not turning a feather. "From what Kraken's told us the Wastelanders have come a long way since they left us. They're reorganised and are stronger than ever. It's only a question of time before they come here again, but they'll have us all prisoner the moment we set foot near their Tunnel. That's precisely what's happened to Quill and his friend, I fear."

"You're right," confirmed the raven. "We had a visit in the Meadow from some minkfolk Black Wood way. They always were scoundrels, and they've joined the Wastelanders. They tried to frighten us by telling us what the Wastelanders had done to Quill and Dink, then they said Mungo would be master of Domusland before the year was out."

"Not over my dead body!" growled Horatio, looking most unusually fierce.

"Nor mine either!" said Big Bill Badger. Then all the animals added their support.

"There must be some way we can stop him, some way we can drive the Wastelanders from Domusland," added Rachel Water-Rat.

"We did it before," said Olive Otter, "and we can do it again, can't we, girls?" she added, turning to her sisters and the vole.

Hoot, however, said not a word. He sat back patiently, blinking wisely and clearly thinking hard. At length he gave one of his meaningful, soft hoots.

"I think Hoot would like to say something else," said Frisk, calling them to order.

"It seems to me," began the owl quietly, "that we need to work out a plan of campaign. First, we must have data . . ."

"Please," said a little voice from the other end of the table, "please, Mr. Hoot, what's a data? I don't know what it is."

It was Fenella Fieldmouse, not a very old little animal, who spoke.

"You're quite right to ask," smiled the owl, looking down at her encouragingly. "One must never be ashamed of confessing one's ignorance. That's how you learn. Parading it, however, is quite another matter. Now then, what *are* data you ask?" The owl put his wing-tips together and closed his eyes as he thought out the right answer. Then he opened them and said quickly. "Data are quantities, conditions, facts, or other premises, given or admitted, from which other conditions or results may be deduced. Satisfied, my young lady?" he concluded, beaming at the young mouse through his glasses.

"Thank you," came back a small, bewildered voice; so small it was barely a whisper.

Horatio thought it was time he came to the mouse's aid—and one or two older animals, too.

"Data are facts," he said kindly, "facts we must have before we can work out our plan."

"Oh!" said Fenella, and "Oh!" said one or two other voices.

Hoot merely blinked and went on, "We must have data, and perhaps Kraken can supply us with them, so that we can all put our thinking caps on—or," he said, looking hard at the fieldmouse, "whatever it is we put on instead. We would be grateful if you could let us have as much information as you can about what's happened to Quill and what's going on. Then we can build up a picture on which to plan our campaign."

Kraken cleared his throat and pushed his specs thoughtfully up his beak and looked very knowledgeable. He liked to be thought wise—and he liked to talk. "Well, ladies and gentlemen," he began as though addressing the Meadow Moot, of which he was chairman, "the Tunnel the Wastelanders are building goes under the Mystery Marshes right into the heart of Mungoville, the capital of Wasteland. Now it so happens I know something of Mungoville. I had occasion to land there in the autumn. I was on my way back from Humanland, where some cousins of mine live in a most ancient Tower in a place called London. It's long been the haunt of a branch of my family, which, as you know, goes back into the mists of time. Now this Tower was a place where kings and queens were executed in the olden days by having their heads struck off. Not the happiest of ways to end one's days headless, I must say . . . but they're strange creatures those humans . . ."

"Tu-woo!" coughed Hoot, cutting the raven short.

"But I'll tell you all about them another day," said Kraken, taking the hint. "Well, to continue. I was on my way back from Humanland, when a most horrible smog developed as I was flying over Wasteland. Their factories and mills simply belched out the filthiest fumes you could imagine. It was terrible! It became so thick and went up so high I couldn't fly over it. I had to land and walk. It was like flying through thick, smelly glue, and it wasn't any better on the ground. It was vile. There were no trees, no hedgerows, barely any grass. Just acres and acres of rubble and cinders, spoil-heaps and slag."

"Did you see Mungoville at all?" asked Hoot.

"I did, indeed. I had to walk all the way across it. I do believe that if I hadn't have held my handkerchief over by beak, I'd have choked to death. I was terrified, too, that I'd be recognised as an outsider and arrested. Police rats were everywhere, but fortunately it was dark and dismal, no one bothered to look at anyone else. They were all too busy hurrying to get off the streets. Such streets; blacker and grimmer than anything I've seen . . . and I've seen some pretty grim streets in Humanland, I can tell you."

"Did you notice anything that would help us in our plan of attack?" asked Horatio.

The raven croaked a little croak, pushed his glasses to the top of his head, and thought hard. "Yes, I did notice something, something very dreadful. There's a large group of buildings right in the middle of the city. It's the prison where they keep all the animals as slave labour. There are two high fences round it, and it's well guarded. There were stacks of guards around when I passed. I had a good look at it, as well as I could, for it was dark even in the middle of the day with all that smog."

"I don't suppose you could draw some sort of plan of it we could work on, could you?" asked Hoot. "Or better still, I wonder if you would come along to Owl View with me. I have a little map-making gadget there, which in next to no time can get out a very accurate map. All you've got to do is to talk to it and Mat will draw you a map. A cartographical concoction I computerised during an idle moment's doodling." The owl hooted modestly. "Doodling goes deeper than you think, you know. Once we've got a map, the plan of campaign will draw up itself."

The other animals agreed. Hoot was such a wise fellow, and they all felt very proud of him in the Great Beyond. There are some folk who are knowledgeable and some who are wise. Hoot was both. He came from a long line of learned owls which stretched right up his family tree, as Kraken was soon to discover.

"Well, folks," said Horatio at length. "I fear there is not much we can do till Hoot and Kraken have compiled the maps we need. We'll meet here again tomorrow at noon, and please come fully equipped for Wasteland . . . blogging-sticks and all! I must confess," he added with a growl, "I'm rather looking forward to meeting Chairman Mungo Brown. Nothing will please me better than to knock the fellow off his chairman's chair once and for all!"

Chapter 6

O wl View was much as it had been when Quill had tumbled into it, the day he had been pursued by soldier rats years before. However, there had been many additions since that memorable day. Hoot was an inventive genius, full of bright ideas he just had to put into practice or machines. Inventiveness does not stand still, and Hoot's inventive mind was never static. Though he sat stock-still for hours on the balcony on the south side of his house, the north end of his head was forever on the move. Behind those wise, slow-moving eyes there was a sharp brain which regarded the world beyond his spectacles with quick precision. Like all wise folk, he said nothing when he was thinking; and he never spoke before he thought.

His home stood in the middle of the Wood, some distance from Fitzworthy Castle. While the other animals went off to pack their bags, Kraken returned with Hoot to Owl View. There he helped Hoot draw the necessary maps by telling him, or rather by telling one of his robots, all he knew of Wasteland and Mungoville.

As they approached Owl View a door opened automatically in the oak tree's trunk. It looked a deceptively ordinary tree, but in reality it was an extraordinary mixture of laboratories, workshops, a massive library, and home,

Kraken approaching Owl View with Hoot

the home in fact of generations of scholarly owls. The old raven croaked in surprise at the sudden aperture which confronted them. His spectacles slid to the very tip of his beak, where they balanced dangerously before he pushed them back.

"Electronic eye," Hoot explained casually. "We broke its beam a few steps back and it opened the door."

"Oh," said Kraken, peering all around him as if the place was full of hidden eyes, then he waddled into Owl View after Hoot. The door slid noiselessly back into place, adding to the raven's discomfort. It was dark, so the owl lit an old lantern. Its yellow beams revealed some sort of entrance hall, at the end of which was a stout, oaken door studded heavy with nails. An army couldn't have battered that down, but it creaked back easily enough on its ancient hinges when Hoot turned the key and opened it.

"I like to blend the old with the new," he said. "I like my roots in the past, though I'm always dabbling in the future. Life would be intolerable if everything were new. I'd hate it. It's all a question of balance. Like ourselves, I suppose. We've come from the past to where we are now. Goodness knows where we'll end in the future, if, indeed, there ever is an end. But it's nice to know the past. Better still to live in it a bit, reassuring. That's why I keep this old door exactly the same as it was in—let me see—yes, in my great-great-great-great Uncle Ulu's time. He was a brilliant chemist, discovered the rare gas Ulumium, you know. They named it after him."

"Er-yes," said Kraken vaguely. Then he thought he'd better come clean. "I must confess though that I know little about science. It's all moved so rapidly since I was a boy. Quite out of my depth with it now—in fact, I always was."

"Just so, just so," said the owl. "It has moved too rapidly sometimes, I think; more than we can cope with. But you can't hold back progress—if that's the right word.

It all depends how you *use* science, not on what you discover. And I shouldn't worry yourself about not knowing much science. There's scores of subjects I'm dismal at—but science—" here the owl's face became rapturous, "science, beloved science has been dear to the hearts of my family for generations. 'Et scientia augebitur'—that's a language called Latin," he explained, "the motto of my College. We owls appear on its coat of arms for we were founder-fathers. It means, 'And so our knowledge is increased.' Ah, delightful days, the days of one's youth! They pass too soon, alas." And Hoot gave three or four soft tu-woos and his eyes became dreamy.

He was aroused from his daydreams by a loud, robot voice calling, "Tea's ready, sir!"

It startled Kraken, but simply took the dreamy look from Hoot's eyes and cut short his tu-wooing. "Won't be a moment, my dear fellow," answered the owl to someone, something up the stairs. "Keep it on the boil. There's a good chap."

"Very good, sir," came back the automated reply, and a more politely automated reply I've never heard.

"My tea-robot," the owl explained, something he was always having to do in Owl View. "He heard us come in and automatically put a pot on the boil. He was programmed to do it ages ago, and old habits die hard. The moment I enter he makes tea. He's turned me into an addict, I'm afraid, but there's one or two things I'd like you to see before we have our cuppas."

And there were many things Kraken wanted to see before they'd gone much further into the house. As they mounted the great, spiral staircase to Hoot's study, they passed all kinds of fascinating rooms, between which, at intervals up the staircase, were portraits and photographs of Hoot's famous ancestors, scholars all of them, scientists and inventors who'd contributed much to 'positive knowledge' —Hoot's term for knowledge which had benefitted the

56

world. Quite the opposite from the negative stuff Mungo Brown's minions scribbled off their drawing boards; or the poisonous filth they bubbled from their laboratories; or the deadly machines they rolled from their engine sheds—all designed to bring misery into life but put more wealth into Mungo's pockets. The Hoot family's inventions had benefitted the world as far afield as Humanland, home of those strange creatures that shared their world but not their life.

Hoot's house was a bewitching place. Through door after door came strange, scientific noises and smells. A propellor whirred in one room and an engine hissed quietly in another. Electronic apparatus hummed away soothingly in yet another. And in each room Kraken caught glimpses of immaculately kept brassware, coils, bottles, tubes, transformers, conductors, reducers, and all manner of magical science gear.

They got to the third floor, and Hoot said, "Let me show you my flying-machine. I believe it's going to come in useful before very long. It crossed my mind we could use it the moment I heard you mention the prison compound and the amount of space there is there."

They entered a very large and very high room, so large it could have been a hangar of some sort, which indeed it was, for there, in the middle stood Hoot's flying-machine. It looked like our own aeroplanes but was much more original. Little knobs and wires stuck out all over the place. It had an adjustable fuselage, a telescopic body which, at the press of a switch, could transform the machine into a single-seater aircraft; or, at the flick of another switch, could extend the bodywork into a twenty-seater passenger plane. There were pedals underneath the seats. "Another idea of mine," said the owl modestly, "to conserve fuel—or to use in an emergency if the normal fuel supply runs out."

"What do the pedals work?" queried Kraken.

"Why," replied the owl, "almost everything. You see, it's my belief folk are becoming far too lazy. We have perfectly good bodies, marvelously constructed machines we operate all day and night, and they last a lifetime; not a minute more nor a minute less. We get them free with ourselves, so to speak; so why don't we use them more and save ourselves a lot of worry, time, and energy we waste on other machines? Why let them idle away when with a little exercise they can do so much good? So . . ." he said, climbing into the cockpit and pulling the raven in after him, "if I want to switch to animal-power, I simply cut off the engine-power here." And he pointed to a button on the control panel. "The flying-machine can be worked entirely by landfolk not blessed with wings like us. All they have to do is simply pedal, and their efforts will turn the propellors or . . ." and here he pulled a lever which made four great helicopter blades open ". . . or they can hover silently above whatever place they want by working the 'chopper' blades with their feet." He pulled the lever again to retract the four blades, pushed a knob, and the flying-machine telescoped from a twenty-seater to the single-seater fuselage once more.

"Incredible!" gasped the raven. "However did you think of all that?"

"Oh, it just comes," said the owl. "After a great deal of thinking it just comes, but it's the thinking that makes it come."

The birds left the hangar and went to Hoot's study. This was really a vast library. There were books everywhere, spilling from innumerable shelves onto three long tables and even over the floor at times. The thick carpet made it soundproof, and they crossed to the owl's desk near the window.

"Take a seat, my dear fellow," said the owl, indicating an armchair on the opposite side of the table. Hoot himself went to his swivel-chair by the drawers. "Tea?" he asked.

"Please," said Kraken.

There was a spluttering and a gurgling to the raven's right, which made him jump. He hadn't noticed a tea-robot there when he entered, and almost lost his specs spinning round to see what was happening. He'd barely time to catch his breath when the tea-robot handed him a ready-made cup of tea on the end of a long, levered arm. "Do you take sugar, sir?" said the robot.

"Yes, please," answered the raven, utterly dumbfounded yet fascinated.

"I ought to have asked you," said Hoot, "but I'm not the best of hosts. Fortunately, my robots make up for my lack of good manners. They've all turned out such good creatures, such fine ro-boys," he added, smiling proudly at his invention. A plate of mixed biscuits went next to Kraken, then with a faint hiss the robot retired discreetly into his alcove.

Dunking a biscuit in his tea, Hoot sorted thoughtfully through some papers on his desk. "Now," he said, "if we can find out where I put my cartography robot, Mat, we can begin drawing some sort of map of the Wasteland prison to get our friend Quill out of it. Now where did I last use Mat?"

"I'm here, sir," crackled a voice from behind another panel in the wall. It slid back to reveal Mat.

"Ah!" said Hoot. "I'd forgotten which alcove I'd put you in. I remember now. I programmed you with a memory bank the last time I used you. I'm becoming more and more absent-minded the older I get," he commented to Kraken. "So I'm building memory banks in all my robots."

The raven simply gaped. He was finding it difficult to gather his aged wits together after all their surprises. Robots, memory banks, tea-machines, and their like had never entered his life before. He turned the conversation to books. He could handle those and felt on safer ground.

59

"You've a tremendous number of books here," he said. "You must know an awful lot if you're read them all."

Hoot looked up and smiled. "Read them all? Oh, no, I only wish I had. But then it's just as well perhaps I haven't. I always make it a golden rule never to believe half of what I read in books. The other half is sheer fiction; sometimes worse. Sometimes it's outright lies."

The raven nodded thoughtfully. Then he said quietly, "A clever person may know everything that's in a book; but the wise one knows which half the truth's in."

"Tu-woo!" exclaimed the owl. "Just so, just so!" and old Kraken by that one observation went up no end in the owl's opinion. "Now, my dear Kraken, if you'd tell Mat, my map-robot here, what you saw around Mungoville Gaol, he'll draw up something in a jiffy."

Kraken looked a bit uncertainly at the microphone the robot suspended before him from one of its arms. "Please speak accurately and clearly," said the machine, which had rolled silently out of its recess, "then I can draw the map accurately. I blur my lines if you blur your speech. When the green light starts flashing, begin to speak." A red light then lit up on top of the machine as a drawing-board slid out of its middle. Two, stainless-steel arms with map-pens attached to them came from the side of a box by the drawing-board on which was a blank piece of paper. On it the robot drew a scale, after first decorating the edges of the map as they used to do in the olden days. Like all else in Hoot's house, the past was firmly embedded in the future and present. "Give me details of what you saw on the outside, then we'll work inwards," said the robot. A green light started to flash when the red one went out.

Kraken cleared his throat rather noisily, making Mat shake. An arm appeared and readjusted the volume control to a lower key, "Sorry," said the raven. "I didn't mean to alarm you."

60

"Don't mention it, sir," said Mat. "My fault entirely. I'd forgotten to set the volume. Gave myself quite a turn inside when you coughed."

The raven then began to tell the machine all he'd seen on the day he'd landed in Mungoville. Swiftly and accurately, before his amazed eyes, a beautiful map began to appear, with ornate compass points drawn in one corner and exotic birds decorating the title. It was a masterpiece of calligraphy and cartography all in one—a Saxton and Speede combined—yet so quickly and so modestly drawn up; Mungoville revealed as it never was in real life, for a map can never disclose unpleasantness in the way a photograph can. Yet it was Mungoville and its gaol; of that there was no doubt, and the raven stood and wondered.

"Well, I never!" he gasped, scratching the bald patch on the top of his head.

"Negative," answered the machine.

"The robot means he can't reproduce 'Well, I never!' on his map. You see, Mat's programmed to draw maps only, not record speech," explained the owl, switching off the machine and thanking it for its work. That done, the robot passed him a newly sketched map, withdrew its drawing-board and arms, then slid silently back into its recess.

Hoot took the map to his desk and examined it carefully, poring over it several minutes before he spoke again. At length he said, more to himself than Kraken, "I think I have it. I believe there is a way to airlift Quill from his incarceration."

"You mean we can help him escape?" asked Kraken. Hoot's big words were sometimes too much for him—and other folk.

"I mean exactly that," Hoot replied. "Now if you'd care to come round to my side of the desk, I'll show what I've got in mind. No, there's no need to get up, my dear fellow. Simply press the blue button on your chair and the chair will do the rest."

61

The raven did as he was bid, and the chair rolled smoothly to the owl's side. If it had taken him to the moon and back, Kraken would not have been surprised. He was quite resigned now to any gadget appearing and doing anything the owl asked. Once he was by Hoot's side, the owl took a pencil and pointed to the map, to the compound where the prisoners exercised in Mungoville Gaol. "If only we could smuggle someone in there to release Quill," he said, "we could lift him out in my flying-machine, but we need someone on the inside to coordinate his escape. I think I know who's just the one to do it, too, once I've finished with her and given her a few lessons in what to do."

"Who may that be?" asked the raven.

"Rachel Water-Rat," Hoot answered. "She knows a thing or two about the Wasteland rats and their police. They had her locked up for months when they were here. She's impersonated them many a time since at parties and such like. She can take them off to a 'T.' They'll never suspect her." The owl looked thoughtfully at his map again. Then the ghost of a smile spread across his beak. "Tu-woo," he said, looking more and more pleased with himself. "And if Rachel could lock up the rat garrison a while, it'll give us time to complete the second part of our mission."

"I didn't know there was a second part," said Kraken.

"Neither did I till just now," said the owl, "but it has occurred to me that we might as well do the job properly and topple that impossible feline Mungo Brown from his perch again. We've to stop him taking over Domusland, if it's the last thing we do. And it certainly won't be that. I've too many inventions not quite finished to allow that to happen." The owl went silent for a while, so silent and so long that Kraken began to wonder if he'd dozed off. Kraken was brought from his own thoughts, which animals always lapse into when their friends are otherwise occupied, by the owl's exclaiming, "Eureka! I have it!"

"Have what?" asked Kraken, looking all about him.

"Mungo Brown—by his mangy tail!" explained the owl. "We'll blow up the Tunnel! We'll unplug the Mystery Marshes!"

"A-a-ah," croaked the raven. "I begin to follow you. You're going to blow a hole in the Tunnel and seal it off. What a brilliant idea! But how?"

The owl left his chair and went to one of the tables which was smothered by rolls of maps. He scrabbled about a moment, then brought back a very ancient-looking map. It was so old, it was brown with age and had crumpled at the edges. Even the piece of string tying it up had gone yellow. Kraken expected it to snap as the owl gave it a tug and spread open the map very carefully. He put an inkwell and two paperweights to hold the map down and stop it recurling. It was a map of Black Wood and the Mystery Marshes made in the olden days years before.

"My!" exclaimed Kraken, looking over the owl's shoulder. "I haven't seen this map before—and I thought I'd seen every map there was of Domusland."

Hoot looked at the back of the ancient map, where an ancient, mouldering, sale number, dried out and dirty, hung by the merest hint of ancient glue. They could just make out the words, "Lotte number VII. Ye olde mappe of ye Black Woode and ye Marshlande of Domuslande, 1746."

"A little item one of my ancestors obviously picked up at a sale. He guessed it would come in handy one day, and time, as ever, has proved him right," said Hoot, blowing a cloud of dust off its surface. "Now, where did you say Mungo's bungalow was he built? You know, the whole of the escarpment there, the Lyth, is riddled with old lead-mines."

"Well, I never!" said Kraken. "I'd heard my old grannie talk about underground happenings and things that came out and grabbed naughty, young animals, but I never really believed her. Not when I grew older, anyway. Nobody lives there now, not our side of the marshes. She was right after all then."

"Of course she was," said Hoot, glancing up. "Old folk generally are—really old folk, that is, and not those pretending to be. What we want to know now is where exactly Mungo has built his bungalow."

"Now let me see," said the raven, stroking his beak thoughtfully. "When I was flying across Black Wood the day I left Mungoville, I think it would be about here. Yes, I'm sure. It was right on the edge of the escarpment, near the little coppice there. On your map there's an old windmill marked, but it's long since gone, though the stump still stands and Mungo uses it as a lookout, I'm told. One of his rats took a potshot at me with his gun as I passed and thought it was funny."

"Sick folk have sick humour," commented the owl. "But his rats will laugh on the other sides of their mean faces before we've done with them. We can reach his bungalow from below, under the ground, and Mungo won't have a clue where we've come from. We'll nab him from under their dirty noses—and once we have him in our hands, it will be relatively simple to make him order his men out of Domusland before we blow up the Tunnel. The Mystery Marshes will do the rest."

"An excellent plan," said Kraken, by now quite excited. "When do we start?"

"Now," said the owl, gathering up his maps. "We'll return to Fitzworthy Castle and tell the others our plans."

"But . . . but it'll take ages," said the raven. "I mean, we can't fly carrying all these maps and things, can we? In any case, it'll be dark soon and I'm not very good at flying in the dark like you owls."

"My dear Kraken," said Hoot, putting a friendly wing round the older bird. "You're forgetting my flying-machine. You will be my first ever passenger—and I couldn't wish for a better. Now, hold onto these maps for a moment, while I programme my robots to look after Owl View when I'm away and I'll be with you shortly. You know your way down, don't you?"

"Of course," replied the raven, who was feeling younger by the moment at the prospect of an adventure—a thought which would have seemed ridiculous an hour before. The years seemed to drop like old feathers from his back as he went down the stairs, two at a time, winking slyly at every venerable portrait he passed; and in the years to come, he always swore that each owl he went by winked back at him.

Meanwhile, Hoot opened the robot-panel on his desk and began pressing button after button, labelled variously "Watchman-robot" or "Cleaning-robot" or Ansaphone-robot," then finally "Memo-robot," which remembered to do any job the owl had overlooked.

Chapter 7

W hile all this was going on, a very sad Quill and Dink, and an utterly despondent pair of magpies, were locked up in Mungoville Gaol. It lay, as Kraken had said, in the black heart of a black city. It was simply a drab collection of concrete buildings, surrounded by a high, electric fence. Each day the four prisoners along with scores of others were taken to different parts of Wasteland to work as slave labour. Their work was bad enough, the dirtiest jobs over the longest hours with the worst food; the usual lot of slave labourers everywhere. However, because Quill years before had fallen foul of the rat warder in charge of his block, the lives of the quartet were made doubly miserable.

They were given the most horrid jobs and made to work the longest hours. They lugged load upon load up and down the Tunnel chained to wagons till they dropped. And as if that wasn't enough, once they had sunk exhausted in their cells at the end of each day, the rat warder who particularly hated Quill would come down and mock them.

He was a one-eyed rat, a scurvy fellow with the number "187" on his shoulder-tag. Nero Squinks was his name, derived it appeared because in the days when he had his full quota of eyes, there was a decided squint in them.

That squint had been passed down generation by generation, but in the way words become altered, the surname of the Squints, as they were at first called, had changed to Squinks, and Squinks it remained to the time our friend inherited it. The quota of eyes he had been blessed with at birth had suddenly been halved in a drunken brawl with another rat. His remaining eye remained firmly lodged in its corner, but over the other a villainous patch had been placed.

His mother had spoiled him enormously. You see, he was her only child and she'd held out great hopes for him. She called him Nero because she enjoyed violins and hoped he would have been a violinist one day. But Nero wasn't really the right build. His musical inclinations lay in other directions. He fondly imagined he had a fine voice which would take him into grand opera if he practised hard enough. It almost took him elsewhere—to the place where all bad singers end their days.

Really, his voice was indescribably bad. Even trying to tell you in words what it was like would give me a migraine, so I won't try. I'll hint at it. It was like a fingernail being scraped over the bottom of a rough saucepan; or it had the screech of one of those frightful pieces of chalk which skirl over the shiny surface of a blackboard making your teeth want to drop out. The combination of a squint and a squeak of gigantic proportions when he sang also suited his name, Rat-warder 187, Squinks, N.

During the time when the Wastelanders had occupied the Great Beyond, Squinks had risen to the rank of rat driver. He had actually been in charge of a horse and cart, and one of his jobs had been to take a load of arms and ammunition to Fitzworthy Castle. But a little episode at the Hilltop Inn, a mile or two outside the castle, when Quill, dressed as a farmer's wife, had tricked the driver so that his cart had rolled down the hill into the river, had left the driver feeling very sore indeed.

He'd been punished greatly by Mungo Brown for neglect of duty. He'd been beaten by his fellow guards. Worst of all, he'd been demoted, shamed in the eyes of his fellow rats and scoffed at by all and sundry. He was now a rat warder, and as such, he had met Quill again. How he tormented him and his friends now! He came each evening and spent hours insulting them and jibing at them. You see, he'd nothing else to do. All the other rats avoided his company—and his voice.

Down he came one night, swinging his staff, then banging it along the doors and windows of each cell, just to annoy any prisoner who was settling down for the evening. A huge bunch of keys hung from his waist, and he jangled them loudly as he strolled along, jeering through cell doors at intervals. Quill heard him coming, and his heart sank.

"Oh, how I wish the miserable animal would go away and leave us in peace," he said to the others.

"Let's pretend we're asleep," suggested Dink.

"Let's pretend we're not here," said Mack.

"I've been trying to do that ever since we came!" wailed a most sad voice from the furthest corner of the cell, where Mick the Thin lay huddled.

Nearer and nearer came Rat-warder Squinks, till at last he stopped outside their cell. The cell had two doors to it. The outer was a solid, metal door. Inside that was a grill-door which gave the warders a better view of the prisoners. The rat opened the outer door and leered at those inside. Quill pretended to be dozing on his bench. Dink stood up and looked out of the window, ignoring Squinks. The magpies hunched themselves into two untidy bundles of feathers and hid their heads. Then the rat rapped sharply with his staff on the rails of the inner door, laughing coarsely when he saw them all jump.

"He, he, he!" he squeaked. "I thought that would make you all sit up! And how have my four beauties been behaving themselves today? It's no use pretending to be asleep or looking out of the window. I'll have you all outside in the cold doubling round the yard till suppertime if you don't listen. Stand up Prisoner 23071618 and answer me!"

Quill got wearily to his feet. He'd learned from bitter experience not to cross the one-eyed rat too often. He was a most vindictive rat and had already seen they had been punished for being sullen or disobeying him. It was no joke having your food cut down or being made to run round and round the yard outside when it was cold and you were tired out. Worst of all, the longer he stayed, the more likely he was to start singing.

"That's better," squeaked the rat. "Much better, I likes to 'ave a bit o' respect when I talks to folk. I don't like being ignored—least of all by prisoners. You got to respect your betters in this life, old prickle-bag, an' don't you forget it. Nah, then, how's it gone today?"

"Not bad," sighed Quill, looking straight ahead and avoiding the leering eye.

"Not bad? Is that all? We'll have to make it better than that. How about 'very good' eh?" sneered Squinks.

"Very good—very good if you insist then," said Quill, trying to humour him.

" 'Ere, you ain't trying to be funny with me, are you, old prickles? 'Cos if you are, I can be funnier," snarled the rat.

"I'm not trying to be anything, least of all funny," said Quill truthfully. "All I want to do is to . . ."

"To what?" asked the rat.

Quill was tempted to say, "To close your silly eye," but he thought better of it, merely saying, "All I want to do is have a little rest. I'm done in."

"He, he, he!" squeaked the rat again, laughing in a high-pitched voice. "I likes it! I likes it! I likes to see you done in. You got me done in once, you fat prickler, an' I'll never let you forget it. No, not as long as I'm out here an' you're in there . . . an' that's going to be for a very long time yet. He, he, he!" he tittered, "Just think, you're never going to see your cosy, little homes again. Leastways out there. This is home now. He, he, he!"

Four groans echoed round the cell. The rat was on good form that night and depressed his audience noticeably. It pleased him hugely.

"You're never, ever going to see your friends either." More groans. "Nor your relations . . ." Still more groans. "Unless you meets up with 'em 'ere." Dead silence, a chilled silence, which amused Nero Squinks so much, he brought on a fit of coughing and had to go off for a drink.

It was just as well, for Quill, Dink, and the two magpies were on the point of hurling themselves angrily at the bars of their cell, but that would have earned them nothing but rapped knuckles and bread and water for a few days. As it was, they held their peace and fumed.

After a time, Mack said, "Has old Bellyache gone yet?" (Mack coined the choicest nicknames for folk.)

"Yes," murmured Quill, sitting down, "but for how long, I don't know."

"He choked himself silly with laughing," said Dink.

"I wish he'd choke himself for good," said Mack. "If ever I get out of here . . ." but his sentence remained unfinished, for Mack—no longer the Fat, by the way—found his anger got the better of him. He was speechless for once and made most bloodthirsty promises to himself of what he'd do to Nero Squinks when and if he became free.

"We'd best try and sleep before he comes back," said Mick—by now the very Thin. "He may keep us up hours once he returns."

"Good idea," said Dink, and the four laid their weary heads on their benches to sleep.

They'd barely got their heads down when, "Psst!" came through the cell window from the exercise yard beyond.

Mack looked up. There seemed to be one of the women rat guards, who patrolled outside, peering in. She wore dark glasses, and her high-peaked cap was pulled well down over her eyes. Rachel was a past-master at disguise, for she'd worked as a secret agent against the Wastelanders when they'd occupied the Great Beyond years before. She knew a great deal about prisons for she and Vicky Vole had spent some time in one after their arrest.

"Psst!" she hissed again, casting a hurried glance over her shoulder to make sure no one was looking, for rat guards were forbidden to speak to prisoners. Mack sat upright, not quite understanding what was happening.

" 'Ere!" he said to the others. "There's one of those blooming women guards trying to talk to us."

"Tell Quill Hedgehog I want to speak with him—quick! There's nobody about here, I may not get another chance," said the stranger in an urgent whisper.

Quill himself heard and sat up, puzzled. Then, as the rat guard lifted her cap a moment to let the light fall on her features, the hedgehog gasped, "Why! It's Rachel Water-Rat! What are you doing here?"

"By prior arrangement with some interested parties from the Great Beyond," she smiled back, "I'm trying to free a certain hedgehog and his friends. Now listen carefully. That one-eyed rat will be back soon and I don't want to let him catch me speaking to you."

A door banged down the corridor even as she spoke. Squinks was on his way back.

"Do hurry. He's coming!" said Quill.

"Tonight we're going to spring you out of here. Squinks has a master-key. Get it from him as he stands by the door. He's a very careless chap, full of his own importance. If you can get him to stand near the door within reach, you can grab his keys from him. When you've got them, throw them out here. I'll do the rest!"

71

"It'll be a pleasure," said Mack. "Please leave this to me, gents both," he said to Quill and Dink, "and I'll show you a trick of the burglaring trade."

Rat-warder Squinks' footsteps drew nearer. His tuneless whistling reached their cell and stopped. The magpie strolled innocently to the door. He smiled at the rat and said, "Mr. Squinks, sir . . ."

The rat's eye gleamed suspiciously at this unexpected politeness, and for one moment poor Mack thought he'd smelled a . . . whatever rats smell when they become suspicious. But he kept his nerve and went on, "Mr. Squinks, I'd esteem it a great favour, sir, if you'd render us one of your little songs before you goes. One of your very own songs. It would make my night."

The others in the cell could scarcely believe their ears. Even Mick, who'd heard Mack tell some whoppers in his time, paled at Mack's words. He was actually inviting that tuneless rodent to sing!

The rat glowed visibly. He loved making up songs, and at least once a week, he'd come to their cell to inflict upon them some terribly ditty he'd composed. The verse was bad enough, but the tunes were worse. And worse than either words or tune was his voice. It was, as I've explained, enough to set your teeth on edge—even false teeth!

Nero thought differently. Like his Roman namesake, he considered himself a genius. Unlike the Nero of history, he'd set nothing afire with his music. On the contrary, whenever he sang, a damp, clammy, sickly feeling fell upon all who heard him. Beads of perspiration, tears of agony appeared at his first, terrible notes. It was monstrous! That was why Quill, Dink, and Mick looked shocked when Mack made his suggestion.

"Why," said Squinks with an oily smile. "I'm pleased to hear that at least one of you has an ear for good music."

And he was so carried away with himself that he released the bunch of keys he carried, and it swung carelessly at his waist. He fumbled in his pocket seeking a crumpled sheet of paper on which he'd jotted his song. "It just so happens when I was sipping my mug of tea last night, before I retired to my slumbers, that the Muse came to me—and I stayed up half the night composing this little song." Here he passed a skinny paw over his brow and closed his eye blissfully after the manner of all poets, particularly bad ones. Then he opened his solitary eye which now had a dreamy, faraway look in it.

"I call this number 'Rat Lullaby.' It's a soothing, little piece."

He cleared his throat. Then it started. At the first note all four prisoners winced. Mack closed his eyes in pain a moment, then opened them and pasted a set expression on his face, trying to look as if he was enjoying it. He didn't want to arouse Nero's suspicion, you see. The others sank into themselves. It was all they could do in self-defense. They put their paws over their ears and Mick hid his head under his wing. As for Nero, the longer he sang, the less he became aware of his surroundings. He was in another world. So was his audience; but a very different world from his.

Squinks sang louder and louder. He drew nearer and nearer to the cell door, and Mack edged his way nearer to the unsuspecting warder. He deserved a medal for his courage. The racket was appalling! Each time Nero hit a high note, he would stand on the tips of his toes and let rip with the force of a fire-siren. His one eye shut tight and his thin mouth opened wide, revealing a very leathery and energetic pair of tonsils, twanging from side to side as the sound waves hit them on the way out.

Mercifully, he reached the last verse:

73

"Sleep, my pretty one, sleep,
May sweet slumbers waft you deep,
Into the world of sugared dreams,
Of chocolate drops and jars of creams,
Where fancy's fragrant fruit-trees grow,
And eggs for eating, row on row,
And all that rats desire to please
Be yours this night in dreamland's ease . . . !!!"

The last word 'ease' should have ended on a very high note, but it came out in a sort of gurgling choke. A black and white wing had come deftly through the cell bars when Nero had got close enough. It caught him by the throat and dragged him against the door. Another black and white wing, equally deftly, found the key-ring round his waist. In a trice, it had been lifted and flung back into the cell behind Mack. Nero continued to gurgle, and his one eye popped alarmingly.

"Open the door and let's 'ave him inside," yelled Mack.

Quill had picked up the keys the magpie had hurled behind him. He dragged his ball and chain to the door and unlocked it. It swung open bringing the half-throttled rat in with it.

"Now then, my fine fellow, now then. I've waited a long time for this," said Mack with great relish as they formed a tight, hostile circle round the terrified rodent. "Would you mind repeating all the complimentary remarks you was making about us earlier this evening?"

Nero gulped, partly to restore his adams apple to its usual place, from which Mack's neck-lock had displaced it; partly because he was so frightened. He was speechless. Beads of sweat ran down his brow, and his eye rolled round and round its socket like a crazy ball-bearing.

"Oh, dear! Oh, dear!" was all he could muster. Then falling to his knees, he gasped, "Please, sirs, I didn't mean

*Rat-warder Squinks begs for mercy after
being taken prisoner by the prisoners*

it . . . I was only joking . . . I was . . ." and a very sickly smile slid over his face. So frightened was he that his patch over the missing eye flapped up and down at each shake of his head.

"What shall we do with 'im, guv?" growled Mack, who couldn't resist giving Squinks the odd cuff to calm him down. "Shall we tear 'im in two?" The smile became sicklier and slid completely off the rat's face.

"Oh, no!" he pleaded. "I'll do anything . . . give you anything . . . only spare me!"

"Tie him up," ordered Quill, "and then fix these on him. They should keep him quiet for a while. Long enough for us to get away."

He pointed to the heavy chains they'd unlocked from their legs and wrists. It didn't take two minutes for the magpies to fit them all on the unfortunate Squinks who sank beneath the rusty iron. Mick took a handkerchief from the rat's pocket and was about to gag him, when Mack said, " 'Alf a mo. I want to make this geezer eat his own words. I want *him* to know what it feels like to 'ave his blooming song rammed down inside you like I had it." And without more ado, the magpie took the grubby sheet of paper on which Nero had written his song, folded it neatly in four, then posted it in the rat's mouth. Mick made sure it couldn't get out by tugging his mouth tightly shut with the hankie.

"There," said Mack looking highly satisfied with his work, "that should keep his horrible mouth shut for a while—an' I hopes his music gives him toothache!"

Quill dumped the rat in the furthest corner of the cell and left him there, a heap of rattling chains on which one terror-stricken eye rolled. Muffled gulps emerged at intervals from this heap as the paper softened in Nero's mouth and slowly disintegrated.

Then the four sat down to wait for Rachel Water-Rat. She appeared as the rat guards outside went about lighting the lamps for the night. In her hand she carried a lantern.

"You got the keys?" she whispered.

"Yes—and Squinks, too," came back the reply.

Her lantern flashed a moment into the corner where the wretched rat lay. Nero's one eye told its own silent tale. It closed sadly as with each gulp another line of his masterpiece disappeared, written, marked, and learned, and most definitely digested.

"Let me have his master-key quick," said the water-rat. "I've a deal of locking-up to do before the others land. It won't be long now. Come out as soon as I call you."

They gave her the key, and she went to the mess-hall where the guards and warders ate their supper. All the latter were eating so there was no danger of anyone going to Quill's cell. Nero Squinks had sealed his own doom finally by giving in to his own conceit and being so vindictive. He'd chosen to do late duty to torment his prisoners and sing. No other rat would allow him to sing with them near, so he had to go down to the cells. He wasn't the most popular of fellows with anyone, you see, least of all his own colleagues.

As it was, the warders on duty in the other blocks had already locked up their charges for the night and were lazing about in their room at the end of each corridor, playing cards or gossiping. So it was a simple matter for Rachel to go round locking them all in their own blocks—and bolting the doors on the outside for good measure.

Next, she strolled over to the mess-hall. The rats had disgusting table manners, and the noise they made when eating was frightful. They lounged about, some with their feet on the table, slurping drink from bottles or cans, and spooning food in as fast as they could. They spilled a good deal of it in the process, but they didn't care. They simply bullied prisoners to clean up after them and jeered at them as they went about their thankless tasks.

Now, the guards always left their muskets stacked outside the door in racks along one side of the mess-hall. It didn't take Rachel long to scoot down the racks putting a special plug of gunpowder down the barrels, a plug invented by Hoot and called a "back-banger." Then she glanced at her watch.

"Just about right," she murmured, feeling inside her jacket for the Hootaphone, a short-wave radio invented by the owl. One of Hoot's robots, a delightful chap called Charley, picked up the transmission at the other end and passed it on to Hoot who was . . . well, you'll never guess . . . who was already in Wasteland along with all the other Great Beyonders. They'd flown in Hoot's flying-machine under cover of darkness to a remote landing strip not far away. Silently, they had glided in an hour before, having switched off the engines and transferred to animal-power, pedalling like mad to keep the propellors turning. Then they'd taken off again for the gaol.

"Hello, hello, is that control?" said Rachel quietly.

"Tu-woo, tu-woo, yes!" said Hoot, scarcely able to contain his excitement. "Come in, Number Three."

"Number Two, sir," corrected Charley from Owl View.

"I mean Number Two, Rachel. Thank you, Charley," said Hoot.

"Number Two to Hoot . . . I mean control," said Rachel. "Everything has gone according to plan. We've got the keys and are waiting for you to land. As soon as you give the signal, I'll flash my lantern and guide you down. Over and out."

"Tu-woo . . . I mean, roger," said Hoot.

"But I'm Rachel," said a bewildered voice.

"Never mind," said Hoot. "I was just being technical. I'll explain later. There isn't tu-woo time now. Oh, I'm so excited . . . tu-woo, tu-woo!"

They had the fuselage on extension, and in pairs behind the owl and Kraken sat Horatio and Brushy, Bill Badger and Frisk Otter, Olive Otter and Leap Hare, the Red Squirrel Twins, and least, but not last, Vicky Vole and her cousin Pippa. Behind them were more otters and young badgers, and right at the rear were four, spare seats for the prisoners about to be sprung.

What a fierce crew they looked! Each had his or her face blacked for camouflage. Each had a weapon, a blogging-stick, a weapon peculiar to the Great Beyond but resembling an Irish shillaly. They didn't use these weapons often, but when they did it was to knock a little sense into their opponents; and many Wastelanders were to become much more sensible folk before the end of this particular operation.

"I think we'd better stay on animal-power," said Hoot. "It will make our entrance all the more effective if we coast in silently. So keep pedalling, ladies and gentlemen, for take-off!"

Hoot turned back to the controls and pulled the lever which operated the helicopter blades. They were heavy, and the crew had to pedal hard to get them turning; but once they started to rotate, the blades were easy to make go faster.

"How's it going?" asked Horatio, puffing madly and pedalling for all he was worth.

"Just a little faster," grunted Hoot, "and we shall be away." He glanced at the rev dial and watched it rise as the crew pedalled more and more furiously.

"I say . . . (puff! puff!) . . ." gasped Olive Otter, "this is just the thing . . . (puff! puff!) . . . for losing weight. I must do it more often . . . (puff! puff!) . . ." And a great drop of sweat trickled off the end of her whiskers.

The blades above whirred faster and faster, then Hoot slipped the machine into gear. It shuddered slightly before taking off straight into the air.

"Tu-woo!" shouted Hoot. "We're away!"

"Ooooops! So's my tummy!" squeaked Pippa's voice at the back.

79

Silently, the aircraft climbed up and levelled out to cross Mungoville. Higher and higher it flew, over grim blocks of tenements silhouetted against the livid light of a nearby steelworks. They went over foundries and factories where workers passed their squalid days before returning through squalid subways to their squalid apartments at night. At times, it seemed as if small volcanoes were spurting out all over the city, where furnaces sent crimson tongues of fire licking at the sky. And everywhere thin chimneys flared orange trailers of burning gas from chemical plants.

"Phew!" remarked Olive, holding her nose. "What a pong! It's like rotten eggs mixed with stale ditch-water. How can they live in air like this?"

Hoot had to press a button at length and let some air-freshener into the fuselage, so bad was the stench. He had to keep his windscreen wipers going, too, to wash away the filth from the dense clouds of smoke.

Thankfully, they were soon over the prison and picked up the signal from Rachel Water-Rat below who guided them safely down. Out they trooped into the quadrangle of the gaol and made for the block where Quill was held. They'd just got to the corner of the block when a voice yelled, " 'Ere! Who are you lot? What you up to?"

A solitary rat guard on sentry-go had turned the corner unexpectedly. He lifted his lantern to have a closer look, then backed away—right into Brushy Fox who had crept up behind him.

"I say, young man, just watch where you're going. You're treading on my toes!" said the fox. Then he blogged the rodent on his bonce before he could sound the alarm. The lantern the rat carried hung a moment, then fell to the ground as its owner went for a brief nap, counting the outer edges of the Milky Way.

On they went, leaving the unconscious rat behind, down to Quill's cell. They had it open in a trice, and the four inmates pattered after them, back to the flying-machine, as quickly as they could. There, Hoot and Kraken awaited them.

"Good show! You managed it all right?" said Hoot.

"Of course we did," said Horatio, falling into the aircraft with all the others, quite out of breath. "It was close though. Let's get out of here before the alarm goes off and they call out the militia!"

The alarm went off sooner than they expected. Someone had stumbled over the unconscious rat they'd sent to bye-byes. A hooter began wailing and searchlights went on everywhere, combing the quad till they picked out the flying-machine. The militia came running through the gates, as from the mess-hall came angry cries and a clattering of muskets being banged against locked doors.

Hoot pulled madly at the starter, but all that came out was a wheezy cough and a half-hearted splutter. He tried again. The same result. And yet again. No luck. The foul air they'd travelled through had choked the air intake. The engines couldn't fire.

"Pedal again!" the owl yelled. "Pedal for all you're worth!" While they were revving the blades, more and more rats poured into the prison from the militia barracks outside. They let the guards out of the mess-hall with their muskets, and a very fat sergeant stood at the door hurrying them out with blows from his cane.

"Get out there an' stop 'em!" he bellowed. "It's more than our lives is worth if that 'edgehog gets away!"

It was a desperate situation. The militia and guards drew nearer and nearer the flying-machine. They'd never seen anything like it, so were afraid it might have something very nasty inside; for rats are cowardly at heart. They gave it a wide berth, but circled it, their whiskers quivering like mad.

As the circle around them tightened, Hoot decided he'd better release his smoke-screen gadget. The nearest rat was a mere twenty metres away, and they were all gaining courage by the second to rush the plane, urged on by their sergeant, still way behind them. In fact, he was right at the back shouting for all he was worth, "Get 'em! You lily-livered lot of squeakers! Get 'em!" Then he rushed along the last line of rats, whacking their shoulders for all he was worth. They pushed forward those in front, who in turn shoved the others.

"All right! All right!" complained the front-liners. "Give us time. We don't know what's in that thing yet. It might go off for all we know!"

In fact, the flying-machine was about to go off. At least the smoke cannister which Hoot had slipped through the door went off. It exploded with a loud bang, and the first three rows of rats thought a bomb had gone off. They fell to the ground in fright, squealing hysterically, their heads under their paws. It saved the day, for it gave the aircraft precious seconds to get airborne. It lifted slowly over the rows of prostrate rats and disappeared into the night.

Stunned at first by the bang and the smoke, the sergeant was dazed; but as the machine rose from the ground and began to fly away, he saw his chances of promotion flying away, too.

"Stop 'em!" he yelled. "Line up in sections and load your muskets!"

The back rows of guards did as he commanded. They also knew what was in store for them if Quill got away, so they lined up quickly and primed their guns.

"Ready! Aim! Fire!" bawled the sergeant—unaware of the back-bangers inside each gun.

Had the volley of shots gone off normally, things might have been very hot for the Great Beyonders. They would certainly have been shot down by a second, but no second volley ever got off; indeed, that first never even left the guns. The muskets bulged in the middle, then blew up! Quill's back-bangers had worked!

82

Never did a sergeant look more surprised. He simply didn't believe his eyes when the rats still on their feet were blown over—with very black faces! He stood puzzled a moment, then looked up as if seeking an answer from the machine just disappearing into the night. He, too, let out a hysterical yell as the smoke from the cannister mercifully hid him from view.

Chapter 8

I t would take too long to tell you how a handful of Great Beyonders in Hoot's magnificent flying-machine threw the whole of Wasteland into panic. Not content with springing Quill and his fellow prisoners, they decided to warm things up before they made their final attack on Mungo's stronghold.

You see, Hoot had studied old maps of Wasteland before they'd set out to rescue Quill, and the more you study old maps, the more your imagination runs riot. So, at the meeting at Fitzworthy Castle they'd all attended, it had been decided they would hide up somewhere after they'd released Quill. From this hideout, they attacked military installations. Hit-and-run affairs to scare the Wastelanders silly. And how they frightened those rats! They were a nervous wreck before a month was out.

Each night the Great Beyonders would fly out from their secret base like a huge dragon. Indeed, many of the Wastelanders swore it was some monster which had come to plague them. Only a few caught glimpses of it, but, as you know, it's the nature of tales, especially horrific tales, to be exaggerated out of all proportion.

Those who did see the flying-machine were late-night workers on their way home, or aged watchmen sitting by their lonely fires in deserted warehouses. They couldn't

Hoot's flying-machine terrifies the Wastelanders

believe their eyes when they saw the Thing fly over them in the stillness of the night. The Thing was the flying-machine with a set of newly painted teeth on the fuselage and a wicked pair of eyes. It was little wonder when those seeing it zoom above, caught in the lurid light of furnaces, fled for shelter or locked themselves in their watchmen's huts.

And in the morning, the rats of Wasteland would discover another target had been destroyed by the Thing which came out of the night. Most of their supply dumps inside Wasteland were unguarded and so were easy targets. Bridges and roads leading to the Tunnel were blown up, till soon the rats were in a turmoil, frightened and becoming more and more rebellious to Mungo Brown.

All this did not help that cat's temper. Remember, he was an alley cat, whose tempers are short at the best of times. The longer the Great Beyonders kept upsetting his invasion plan, the angrier he became and the more and more rats he punished. The more he punished, the less control he had. Some of them became openly mutinous and were clapped in gaol. His Black Jackets alone held together his army by constant bullying and many arrests. Soon, he became the most despised creature in Wasteland— a country where everyone despised everyone else as a matter of course. So you can tell how despised he was.

As you can imagine, he was particularly harsh on Rat-warder 187, Nero Squinks. More and more, that miserable rodent became the object of Mungo's wrath. Each time news of the flying-machine's attacks reached him, Mungo's hatred for Nero Squinks reached blacker depths. And as the cat's hatred blackened, so did the rat's punishments. Poor Nero! Even the other rat warders began to feel sorry for him, and that had never happened before.

His punishment started from the moment the sergeant reported Quill's escape. Mungo had been strolling smugly in the grounds of his flashy bungalow, when one of his

Black Jackets informed him the sergeant was outside. Fondly imagining it was a routine report, Mungo blew out a large smoke ring from his cigar and asked the Black Jacket to send in the sergeant. It delighted the cat to hear how his prison and its inmates were faring. It set him imagining how miserable Quill was every time he had news from the prison, so he was looking forward to hearing the sergeant's report.

Mungo went indoors, handing his coat to a servant. It took him some time to struggle out of it, for he had grown decidedly fat—very fat! His huge paunch with its many-linked, gold chain stretched tightly from one waistcoat pocket to the other, like the cables on an overloaded suspension bridge. His paunch had an existence of its own, for it waddled and shook ages after the rest of him had settled down. It was a most independent paunch!

Yet it had its advantages. It needed a great deal of filling for a start; and filling it provided Mungo with much happiness. He had also developed an endearing habit of butting people with it when he felt annoyed with them; a habit which had grown with the paunch. Many was the unfortunate animal who'd gone sprawling full length when he'd been butted by Mungo in one of his rages.

His stroll left him empty. The cold, too, had sharpened his appetite, rarely blunt at the best of times. He thought he'd just time for a small tin of sardines and a quick gollop of cream, before the sergeant came in. In fact, he golloped his cream first before the sergeant's entrance.

The cream sweetened the cat immensely. It always did. "Oh, do come in, my fine fellow," purred Mungo, waving a sticky paw in the rat's direction. "I'm looking forward to any tale you've got to tell me about our friends in Mungoville Gaol." Then Mungo opened his sardine tin. He was uncommonly uncouth!

The sergeant saluted and clicked his heels smartly. There was a pause. Then he gulped. It was the gulp which caught Mungo's attention as he was about to drop a sardine into his mouth. Instead, he halted, suspending the sardine in mid-air and turning his head. Something in the rat's manner seemed very disconcerting.

"Anything wrong, my good man?" asked the cat.

That ominous gulp surfaced again. The sergeant coughed to try and inject a bit of wetness into his dry mouth. Then he stammered, "I . . . I have to report, sir, that . . . that . . ."

"Well?" said Mungo, the tiniest irritated.

"That . . . that Prisoner 23071618 and his cell-mates have escaped," blurted out the rat.

Mungo's voice took on the hard edge which came whenever he grew angry. "And who is Prisoner 230 . . . whatever the rest of his number is?"

The sergeant began to sweat fearfully, and it took all his courage to get out, "It's that hedgehog, sir. Him as you said had to be particly watched."

The sardine never reached Mungo's tum. It was hurled, along with the rest of the tin, at the sergeant's head. Fortunately for him, the cat's aim was not good. The contents of the tin splodged across the rat's uniform, and the tin went on its travels to the wall behind, clonking to the floor. Sardines and tomato sauce splattered the rat, but being the good soldier he was, he held his ground and stood rigidly to attention. Then Mungo waddled angrily across the room and wanged him with his tummy.

"You blithering blockhead!" he yelled, working his paunch up to another wang which knocked the sergeant onto his back. "Get up!"

The rat got to his feet and came to attention once more. Mungo backed off a pace to get some sort of run at the rodent. Then he started his next onslaught. The paunch came like a tank, the gold chain flailing up and down. The rat closed his eyes and waited.

88

"O-o-ooo!" he wailed. "It wasn't my fault. It was Rat-warder 187's."

"And who's he when he's at home?" asked Mungo, giving the other another larrop with the chain-spangled tum.

"Nero Squinks," snivelled the sergeant, staying on the deck this time where it was safer.

"Not that idiot again!" bellowed the cat as memories of the Hilltop Inn rose like spectres before him. "What happened?"

"No one rightly knows, your honour," said the poor rat. "It was dark. Some great dragon Thing came whir-ring out of the sky. A flying-machine from outer space, it seemed."

"Something from out of your thick heads!" snarled Mungo, turning on his heel after giving the rat a kick or two just for fun. "You'll be telling me pigs have wings next!"

"I don't know about pigs, sir," said the rat, peering from between his hands on the floor, "but this Thing has wings and a great set of teeth. The hedgehog was snatched by black-faced devils what came out of it. They carried blogging-sticks all of 'em—an' we was well and truly blogged!"

"It's those dratted Great Beyonders meddling in my affairs again," said Mungo Brown. "But I'll teach 'em to mind their own business. They'll pay for this when they're caught and catch 'em I will. And once they're in the bag, I'll . . . I'll . . ." but the cat never said what he was going to do. He lashed his tail this way and that, knocking flower pots and ornaments flying whenever he passed the low tables about him. "But first, I'll deal with that one-eyed, nitwit Squinks," he said.

Poor Nero! How he suffered. First he was beaten. Then he was put in solitary confinement in the vilest cell, an evil-smelling cell deep underground, where there was no light and little air and where water trickled down the walls in green slimy trails. His food was black bread and water. He was hung up in chains on that green, slimy wall where all sorts of horrible, creepy-crawly things made their home and found their way across his body during their midnight strolls.

Finally, when there seemed no sign of the Great Beyonders being caught and Mungo's patience was exhausted, the rat was sentenced to death; partly to satisfy Mungo's desire for revenge; partly to act as an example to anyone who rebelled against him, for by now there were many openly opposed to the cat.

One day, Mungo summoned the rat sergeant to his bungalow and flung a piece of paper at him, ordering him to pick it up and read it. He did so and read out:

"Three days from the above date, Rat-warder 187, Squinks N., by express command of Chairman Mungo Brown and the Black Jacket Council, will be taken from the place of his arrest and shot at dawn. Signed Chairman M. Brown & Officers in Council."

"You understand that?" growled Mungo.

"Yes, sir!" gulped the rat.

"It also means that anyone failing in his duty from now on, anyone complaining about my decisions or questioning my orders, will suffer the same fate as Squinks. Is that quite clear? Take that notice and have it posted throughout Wasteland. Now get out!" he yelled.

The sergeant saluted, turned and fled, rushing past the bullyboy Black Jackets who lined the room with folded arms. When he had gone, Mungo turned to the nearest Black Jacket and leered, "That should fix 'em."

The Black Jacket leered back and croaked, "You fix 'em every time, sir, you do. We've never known you not fix anyone. You're the best fixer we've come across."

Mungo grunted. It was the nearest he ever got to saying thank you, and the Black Jacket was pleased. He liked to keep Mungo in a good mood, for the cat rewarded them well. He fed them splendidly from his bursting larder— especially with eggs, best, brown eggs, which rats are particularly fond of.

"Colonel," said Mungo to a much-medalled rat who was never far from him. "Once that idiot Squinks has been dealt with, muster the army. I've decided to bring forward the invasion of Domusland. Those nervous twits out there will soon be in no condition to set foot outside their own doorsteps the way things are, let alone carry out an invasion. We must strike soon. See to it that all units are ready by the end of the week."

"Yes sir!" said the colonel and turned to the major by his side. "Get the militia mobilised for Operation . . . Operation . . ." and here the colonel frowned. He couldn't remember the code name for the invasion. A keen, young subaltern helped him out, as all young subalterns should, for both the major and the captain had also forgotten. "Operation Mystery Marshes, sir," he whispered to the captain.

"Er . . . quite," said the captain. "Operation Mystery Marshes," he repeated to the major.

"Just so," said the major and turned to the colonel to tell him. When the colonel heard it, he coughed and said, "Operation Mystery Marshes. That's it. See to it at once that the forces are mobilised." And the subaltern was sent off to get things going.

Mungo watched the young subaltern, keen for promotion, speed off towards the Tunnel. He purred quietly to himself, a sure sign he was pleased. Then he rubbed his fat paws. "Money, money, money," he murmured seeing in his mind's eye Hedgehog Meadow developed to the last square yard. And the fat pouches under his eyes began to look more like money bags the longer he thought.

Chapter 9

I t was about this time that the Great Beyonders hit a
serious problem. The lead-mines under the Lyth
escarpment were far more complicated than either Hoot
or his map-robot had guessed. It became more and more
clear they needed someone who knew those mines thor-
oughly. But could they find anyone who would dare even
set foot near them? Oh, no.

The Wastelanders were a superstitious lot; worse than
their counterparts on the other side of the Mystery
Marshes, and they were bad enough. All sorts of fright-
ening tales were told about those marshes and mines. Sto-
ries about weird creatures such as Griptoes and Grozzies,
frightful things which haunted the depths of the old mine-
workings and came out only at night to grab anyone
straying too close to their lairs.

The Griptoes were six-legged, giant insects which had
luminous eyes and suckers on their feet. These terrible
pedivacs (to give them their biological name) held you
tight while they sucked dry your blood! The Grozzies,
on the other hand, were more civilised, very like Humanfolk. They had two legs and the usual number of arms
and toes, but, like Nero Squinks, they had one eye. This
was red and set in the middle of their foreheads. It was
for seeing, but it also gave out a beam which paralyzed

you at once, made you grozzy, which is the stage worse than groggy; hence their popular name. Their biological name, however, was soporfacts. Once they'd stunned you, they carted you off underground and put you in cold store till an appropriate mealtime. Then you were defrosted, cooked by microwaves from their eye, and scoffed.

There was, strange to tell, one rat who knew these workings like the back of his skinny paw—the most despised rat in Wasteland; the rat long ago abandoned by any self-respecting Wastelander because of his voice. There's no prize for guessing who he is, but while the others were worrying about their problem, Quill suddenly remembered that his old gaoler used to speak often about the lead-mines. He openly boasted that he had no fear of them and was the only rat who dared enter them. It was the only place he could practise singing, you see. He'd been forbidden to sing anywhere else!

Lacking much imagination, the ancient mines held no terrors for him. In any case, had there really been Grozzies down there, they'd have fled long since once they'd heard him sing. But those same solos he launched, deep down in the mines, only confirmed what the folk living near the Mystery Marshes had always believed. There was something horrible living down there, for they heard it wailing to itself at intervals.

Even bats, which had lived there for generations, abandoned the mines after the first singing practice of Nero Squinks. Bats, as you know, have very sensitive ears and he'd almost destroyed their eardrums by his racket. They'd shot out of the mines, flying for their lives in one, long swarm to the opposite side of Wasteland, making their new home in some old workings there, suffering hang-ups for weeks afterwards.

Once he had the lead-mines to himself, Squinks had started to explore them. In fact, he'd made it his hobby. In no time at all he knew the lead-mines inside out and

Even bats flee from the sound of Squinks' "singing"

spent hours there, rummaging among old machinery and making money on the side selling any scrap metal he found.

"If only we could get hold of Squinks, he'd take us straight to Mungo's headquarters. If we'd known this was going to happen, we'd have brought him with us when you sprung us," said Quill.

Mack the Fat grimaced and shook his head. "He might have sung," he said. "And that would have finished all of us!"

Just at that point, Rachel Water-Rat came in. She was still going regularly into Mungoville under cover, picking up bits of information and generally keeping her eyes open for anything useful to their plans. They'd attacked a warehouse filled with muskets the previous day and blown it up, and they asked her what the Wastelanders' reactions had been. She grinned and took off her hat and the Wasteland uniform, joining them round the table for some of Brushy Fox's soup. Brushy was an excellent cook. Give him a couple of onions, a few vegetables, a dash of herbs, and a bit of game, and he'd dream you up a magnificent soup in no time.

"Perfect!" said Rachel. "Absolutely splendid!" she continued, spooning down great mouthfuls of soup.

"Just as I expected," said Horatio. "I knew our attack on that warehouse would shake 'em."

"I mean the soup, you clod," said Rachel. "Our attack yesterday was merely successful, but this soup is super—if you see what I mean," she added. The others groaned. Rachel was always making puns, but she ignored their pained looks and went on ladling in the soup. When it was done, she licked her lips and said, "I've some rather interesting news for you folks. Old Mungo Brown has sentenced that rat-warder friend of yours to be executed for letting you escape. What's his name?"

"Squinks," growled Mack, wincing at the very name.

"Yes," continued the water-rat, "he's going to have Squinks shot at dawn and what's more, Mungo is going to attend the execution in person. He's had it pinned up all over the place. Trying to frighten the Wasteland army, I hear. They're ready to mutiny, the lot of 'em."

"That puts paid to our lifting Squinks then," said Quill despondently, and a cloud of melancholy fell upon them all.

"I know it sounds daft," remarked Dink Dormouse slowly, "but I feels sort of guilty inside. I wouldn't have wanted old Squinks bumped off on my account."

"Me neither," said Quill.

The two magpies felt much the same. "There's lots of things I felt like doing to old Squinksie," grunted Mack, "but I'd have drawn the line at shootin' the bloomin' croaker."

"Then we must think of some way of saving him," said Rachel, having finished her soup, and the animals gathered round the long table to think as only the Great Beyonders could. They knew that by using combined brain-power an idea would get off the ground, rather like the flying-machine. A sigh left Pippa Vole at the end of the table and passed right along each creature in turn, until it disappeared into the night through Dink who was guarding the entrance. Then a second sigh, an even louder one as their combined brain-power built up, left Dink and came back in reverse order to the little vole.

At this point, Hoot cried suddenly, "Tu-woo! Eureka, I have it! Back-bangers again. That should do it!"

Everyone thought Hoot had gone mad. He startled old Kraken so much his spectacles fell off and clattered onto the table.

"I'm sorry, Kraken," said the owl, as the old bird fumbled short-sightedly trying to find his specs. "But I think I've hit it."

"Hit what?" said Bill Badger rather irritably. He didn't like sudden outbursts, even from enlightened owls.

"How to spring Squinks," said the owl.

"They won't let us get away with it a second time," said Rachel. "They've got cannon manned day and night to stop flying-machines coming in again to the gaol."

"We shall not *fly* into it. We'll *drive* in, in style!" said Hoot.

"You feeling all right?" said the badger, looking more grumpy than ever.

"Perfectly," replied the owl, giving Bill an odd look over his glasses. "In fact, more perfectly than usual—which is more than I can say for some folks."

"Humph!" grunted Bill and turned away. He'd had a tiring time the last few days, and he wasn't a day man at all. He'd missed his sleep badly.

The owl went on, "Now my plan is this. I want Horatio to be Mungo Brown for a while . . ."

"He *has* gone mad!" interrupted Bill, shrugging his shoulders.

"If I may be allowed to continue without further interruption," said Hoot severely, "I will tell you what I have in mind." He looked at Bill, who stared at the ground but said nothing. "You see, if Horatio can impersonate Mungo Brown for a few minutes, we can get Squinks clear by car."

"But where are we going to get a car from?" asked Vicky Vole.

The owl smiled and pointed to his remarkable flying-machine parked outside. "A little touch of paint and a few adjustments and my flying-machine becomes a facsimile of Mungo's limousine."

"A what?" said Big Bill, still ruffled.

"He said it will become like the fat smile on Mungo's car," explained Mack. "Haven't you noticed? His car looks just like him. All cars look like their owners give 'em time."

Hoot ignored Mack's explanation, but went on to show just how they could enter the gaol by Horatio's disguising himself as Mungo and by Rachel Water-Rat and a couple of the otters dressing up as Black Jackets, Mungo's bodyguards.

As for the flying-machine; first, the helicopter blades came off. Then, at the press of a button, the wings telescoped neatly under the fuselage. Another press of a button, and the bodywork contracted to a sleek limousine. Two or three hour's hard work with the paintbrush—and the flying-machine was finally transformed into the Hootobile Mark I.

Other preparations had to be carried out, too. Rachel Water-Rat went into the gaol again and calmly fixed the muskets of the execution squad with back-bangers. (They were brand-new muskets as they put the last fiasco down to the old muskets' age.) Horatio was padded out with cushions by Mack the Fat, a master of disguise. Then Mack schooled Horatio for hours walking, talking, and acting like Mungo Brown. At the end of which, Mack told that worthy aristocrat what a fine alley cat he made. "Your dad himself, old Felinus, would have sworn you'd been brought up in the gutter from birth," said Mack—and got a very old-fashioned look from Horatio by way of reply, I can tell you. By the morning of the execution they were all ready.

As for poor Nero Squinks, they released him from his chains the night before and let him quake on the edge of his hard bunk all night, nibbling his nails right down to the quick. His colleagues tried to cheer him up, but they failed miserably—especially when they had to refuse his last request. He begged him let him sing one last, little song he'd composed. "It's a dirge," he explained.

"A what?" they asked.

98

"A funeral song—*my* funeral song," he explained gloomily.

"You sing?" said the chief warder. "Never! Anything but that, Squinks. I'll face the firing-squad myself first! Besides, you know it's against the law. We can't let you do that."

And that was that. The poor fellow wasn't allowed to sing his own funeral lament, so he sat sadly in his cell all night, quietly shedding the odd tear from his odd eye and nibbling what was left of his nails—a most miserable rat.

The winter night prolonged his agony, for dawn was a long time coming. From time to time, the two guards in charge of him brewed up hot cocoa and he tried to drink that. But the nearer the time drew towards daylight, the more his cocoa was salted by tears, making it undrinkable.

Then about an hour before dawn, a sleek limousine drew up at the gates unexpectedly. Its headlights were blazing, and the Wasteland flag fluttered from its bonnet. A Black Jacket jumped out and showed some official papers to the sentries. At once, the whole prison sprang to life, and rats scurried here and there. A guard of honour was turned out sooner than expected, and twenty, bleary-eyed rats lined up and presented arms as the car left the guard-room and swung through the gates into the top-security block where Squinks was held.

There, a fat sergeant, the very one who'd made such a hash of things before, rushed around whacking the firing-squad for all he was worth. He desperately wanted promotion, and this was his last chance. If he could elevate Squinks to higher levels, he, too, would move up the promotion ladder. "Come on! Come on! You idlers!" he shrieked. "Chairman Brown is here. He's brought forward the time of execution. Trust him to catch us out. If you lot make a mess of it this time, there'll be more than Nero

99

Squinks moving up the queue! Get a grip of yer muskets an' move!"

There was much activity down in the cells, too. Nero was whisked from his bunk and tied up unceremoniously. A nasty Black Jacket marched before him carrying a nastier black hood which they put over his head outside. Two bigger Black Jackets caught him under the shoulders and ordered him to march. He tried. Yes, he tried hard, but his legs went to jelly, so they lifted him up and carried him out.

"Left, right, left, right!" barked the chief warder, once the tiny procession had lined up. All Nero could do was pump his legs up and down in time with the commands, while the Black Jackets holding him did the marching.

They went into the courtyard where the firing-squad stood to attention. All Nero could manage was "Oh, me! Oh, my!" as they carried him to a large post in front of a wall. The black hood was placed over his head and a long rope wound round and round his middle. But for this he'd have slid helplessly to the ground. All that was heard was, "Oh me! Oh, my! Mercy, great Mungo!" coming from the hood.

But the cat with the dark glasses and huge cigar in the limousine turned not a hair. He pressed a button inside the car, and the window slicked down. Then he growled through it, "Carry out the execution! He'll get no mercy from me—nor anyone else who disobeys me!"

The fat sergeant waddled over and saluted with his sword. "We await your command, sir," he greased. The cat nodded and the rat clicked his heels, all very noisily. Then he marched to the six rats stood to attention with their muskets. He stopped at their flank, held his sword high in the air and yelled, "Ready!" The six came up into the firing position. "Aim!" he commanded, and six eyes— one for each rat—closed and lined up behind their muskets. (Nero's eye at the other end of the line closed, too; tight—very tight!) Then "Fire!" screamed the sergeant.

There were six loud bangs. Six very loud bangs. The sergeant's sword cut through the air and pointed at the ground—where six very still and very black-faced rats lay. The back-bangers had done it again.

The smoke cleared, and the sergeant stared in sheer disbelief. He looked first at Nero Squinks, who was very much alive, shouting hysterically from inside the hood something about, "You rotten lot! You missed me! You missed me on purpose! Let me out! Let me out!" Then the sergeant looked at his squad. Not for long. He was blogged as he turned open-mouthed to face the nearest Black Jacket, who was blogged, too, with the others who gaped unwitted.

Squinks also had to be blogged to shut him up. He was cut free from the post and carried to the car which sped to the gate. There, the guard sprang to attention again, and Horatio waved a lazy paw at them, after the manner of Mungo Brown, before they disappeared into the night.

Later, as the dawn streaked icily across the sky, another limousine drew up with the real Mungo inside. What followed I dare hardly relate.

There was utter pandemonium, with rats running wildly all over the place. Once they'd found out what had happened, sirens wailed, hooters hooted, and whistles blew everywhere. Order countered order. Guards were panic-stricken, and the chief officer was still grilling the sergeant when Mungo rolled up. But all the sergeant did was gibber. No one got any sense out of him for hours.

Of course, someone had to tell Mungo, and the sergeant got all the blame. When Mungo heard that Squinks had been rescued, his cigar popped clean out of his mouth. He jumped out of his car so fast he almost left his paunch behind, but it managed to catch him in time to give the sergeant two hefty wangs. Then he seized that shivering mass of rattery by the throat and bellowed, "You let Squinks escape! Why you . . . you blundering, useless bag of rat-wind, can't you do anything right?" And he shook the rat so hard his teeth could be heard rattling back at the guard-room and set the rats there quaking, too.

"Take him away!" snarled Mungo. "Take him to the dungeon Squinks was in. Chain him to the wall and whatever punishments Squinks was on, double them! Once I've completed the invasion of Domusland, I'll hang him over the entrance to the Tunnel where he'll rot his fat brains away. He'll be an example no one will want to follow."

The colonel, the major, and the captain all stood a respectful distance from Mungo, nodding vigorously in agreement with all he said. Finally, when he'd vented his rage as much as he could on the unhappy rat, the sergeant was carted off to the dungeons. Then Mungo shouted at the colonel, "Have all available troops assembled at the mouth of the Tunnel. Tomorrow at dawn, they march to Domusland. I'll delay no longer. We've wasted time enough as it is. I'll wait for you at the Black Wood end of the Tunnel." Then growling angrily to himself and lighting a fresh cigar, he heaved his tummy into the limousine. Once it had settled comfortably down, they drove off.

However, still disguised as a Black Jacket, Rachel Water-Rat overheard all he said. She'd remained behind to see what happened after they'd rescued Squinks. It was just as well she had done, for having listened to Mungo she sped back to their hideout, where the still very distant Squinks was returning to this world from the brink of the one he'd stood at scarcely an hour earlier.

"Where am I?" he asked faintly, opening his one eye slowly, half-expecting to find himself in whatever ratty heaven awaits good rodents. "What happened?" Then he gave a long, "Ooooooh!" as the genial features of Mack the Fat and his blogging-stick came into focus.

"You're all right. We shan't harm you," Horatio reassured him. "We want you to help us now."

The fear in Squink's eye turned to suspicion. He wondered what they were up to, why these former enemies had suddenly become friendly. He looked slowly round the circle of faces surrounding him, starting with Horatio and finishing with a vole. They didn't seem particularly hostile, and his suspicion began to waver. He looked again, starting with the little vole and finishing with Horatio. Yes, he decided, they meant it. They were friendly—even the magpies, though it took a second look at Mack to convince him. They really were friendly, and that was a conclusion he hadn't come to for a long, long time.

"What happened?" he repeated.

Mack cleared his throat and said with great feeling, "You was snatched from the jaws of death. Then you was blogged. Then you was brought here—for your own 'ealth. You don't deserve to be 'ere, but these are true gents an' they risked their lives to rescue you. We didn't like the thought that you was being bumped off on account of us, you see. You oughter be the gratefullest rat alive, Nero Squinks."

He nodded solemnly at the rat, who looked at his boots a moment, as if thinking deeply or wrestling with new feelings that stirred far inside him. Then Nero raised his eye and coughed. "Thank you," he said simply. "Thank you from the bottom of my heart."

Mack rather ungraciously muttered something about not knowing the rat possessed such an organ, but the others ignored him.

Then Squinks went on, "I am truly sorry for *all* my past behaviour." And he looked most soulfully in Quill's direction. Quill, who was a soft-hearted fellow, replied that that was something they'd best forget, and if the rat was really determined to make a fresh start, then the quicker, the better, because they needed his help.

103

"You see," continued Hoot, "we want your expertise, your speleological expertise."

Nero joined everyone else there looking blank. Hoot blinked and sensed they hadn't understood him, but it was Brushy who blurted out, "We want you to help us get under the Mystery Marshes. You know all about the tunnels and mines there."

"That's what I suggested," said Hoot patiently, "though you didn't understand me." And he grumbled to himself about people needing to be more familiar with their own language.

"You see," said Olive Otter, "we're going to capture Mungo Brown and stop him invading Domusland."

"You'll never get near his place," said Squinks. "It's alive with Black Jackets and all sorts of things to stop folk getting in."

"Of course we won't get in if we approach it by conventional routes," said the owl. "But we're not going overground to snatch him. We're going under it."

"Ah, I see," said Nero, and winked his one orb knowingly. "What clever fellows you are. Underground! Brilliant! Nabbed from underneath. He'll never suspect it."

"Exactly," said Horatio. "He'll be expecting us to come at him from the air or on the level. What he doesn't realise is just how suspect the ground is under his very feet."

It was then that Rachel made her entrance and told them about the invasion. "We must carry out our snatch tonight or we'll be too late," said Horatio. "Now, Nero Squinks, you can prove you've turned over a new leaf by leading us to Mungo's bungalow under the Marshes."

Nero's eye gleamed with newfound righteousness. "I can take you directly there without having to set a paw even outside this old pit-head you're hiding in. You see, it links up with the old lead-mines through one of its galleries. I know it well." And here he smiled serenely. "I sang my first practice here. Would you like to listen to

104

the little song I composed then? You get quite a good resonating effect here."

"You keep your blooming singing to yourself!" said Mack quickly. "You'll have the whole blooming roof fall in on us!"

The rat heeded his words. He did not sing, and they all breathed freely. He told them to prepare for the journey under the Marshes. The owl asked what was to be done with his flying-machine, as they couldn't fly it into Domusland openly.

"We can drag it through the passages," said Squinks. "I know where the high ones are. Now, if you put all your gear into it, we can make a start."

"Tu-woo," said Hoot. "I do believe this rodent has really turned over a new leaf and is seeing life through new eyes."

"Eye," corrected Nero. "Yes, I think I must have been looking at life through the wrong eye all these years. New light dawned when you hit me on the head inside that hood. Perhaps you knocked some sense in at last."

And by the gentle light in his eye, they could see he was indeed a new rat. What's more, as well as living a better life from then on, he influenced others to do likewise. But that is another tale.

Chapter 10

Mungo Brown had returned from reviewing his troops at the Wasteland end of the Tunnel, where they had gathered for the invasion of Domusland. Oh, how that alley cat loved his reviews! He was the perfect dictator. They satisfied his self-praise, gratified his love of power, and blew up his ego till he was fit to burst. Oh, how he revelled in the mass hand-clapping, the chants, the forest of stiff-arm salutes in his honour! Oh, how he simply adored strutting up and down beneath the blown-up pictures of himself on a rostrum draped with flags and yes-men! And how he enjoyed whipping up the crowds below into hysteria till they hung on his every word.

But the speech he made that day was to be his last. His army was already seething with discontent, as he had them drawn up before him at the entrance to the Tunnel. The usual cheers were a bit slow forthcoming till the Black Jackets moved in. With the help of a few hints, such as prods from swords and hefty kicks on the ankle, the army warmed up and offered its tithe of adulation. Mungo was moved and after his speech went back to his bungalow on the other side of the Tunnel.

"Yes," he said, sinking into a chair with a sigh, "it's been a tiring day, but what a satisfaction it is to be great." He closed his eyes and drew heavily on his cigar. In imagination, he saw once more the Wasteland army, militia, and police force drawn up beneath him and offering wave on wave of chants and slogans. It was like incense rising to a god. "Tomorrow," he sighed, "tomorrow—oh! the glorious tomorrow! They will march in their thousands past me to glory—and wealth! Domusland will be mine!"

The colonel signalled to the major, who signalled to the captain to take an ashtray to Mungo so that he could knock the ash from his cigar into it. The captain clearly thought it was beneath his dignity to perform such a menial task and pressed the button for a servant, who promptly appeared. The servant was Derry Dormouse, the cousin of Dink. He had been made to wait on in Mungo's house. Cringing under the captain's cane, which he always used on servants, Derry took the ashtray and waited for the cat to drop in his ash. Mungo opened one, sleek eye and saw the dormouse. The eye glinted cruelly and he said, "Yes, Domuslander, this time tomorrow your land will be mine. No more of those ridiculous Moots selected by your peasants. Your land will be run profitably from now on by me."

He closed his eyes again to purr up dreams of towns and cities. Already before him Mungo Crescents and Closes appeared, Mungo Motorways and Terminals. Hedgehog Meadow and Dormouse Dingle simply disappeared under high-rise apartments and brash, boxlike bungalows. He smiled and chortled to himself as he pictured his troops sweeping across green fields and down leafy lanes, over ploughland and through woods, followed by hordes of rats grubbing the countryside into one huge city.

"I've been thinking," he said at length. "We ought to rename Domusland once we've conquered it. What do you suggest?"

The colonel took his cue. He pretended to think hard a moment, then lifted his eyebrows in an oily and self-effacing smile. "What about . . . what about New Mungoland?" he ventured.

"Brilliant!" said the major.

"Fantastic!" said the captain.

"You really think so?" murmured Mungo modestly. "You think it will go well with the people? After all, we must consider the people."

"No doubt at all," said the colonel. "The very first Assembly will give it priority. It will be the first bill the junta will pass."

"New Mungoland," whispered the cat, his eyes now fixed distantly on the ceiling. "New Mungoland," he repeated, absolutely enraptured by the name. "What a beautifully sounding name for a new country, a new era! You dream up the most exquisite ideas, colonel. Take a crate of kippers as a present."

The colonel bowed stiffly. He nodded to the major, who nodded to the captain. He immediately sent off a servant to Mungo's larder to take the kippers to the colonel's house nearby. Then followed a long session of back-biting and boot-licking during which many cheers and many trays of eggs went in the direction of the colonel's residence. Mungo didn't mind. He would replenish his larder from what his troops plundered next day.

So intent was the cat soaking up the flattery with which the rats larded him, and so intent were they at buttering him up, that not one of them heard a faint tap-tap-tap underneath the hearthstone in the grate at the opposite end of the lounge. However, one animal there heard it, Derry, for he was standing out of the way by the hearth. Puzzled, he looked into the fireplace and blinked, as the great slab of stone began to rise, inch by inch. Then three pairs of eyes peered out of the blackness. They looked all round the room, focusing at length on Mungo and his henchmen, who had their backs to the hearth, quite oblivious to what was happening behind.

Mungo's capture about to be effected

The officers were jawing on and on telling Mungo what a fine fellow he was. "You've done a splendid job, sir," said the colonel, cracking an egg from a bowl nearby and drinking it slurpily.

"Absolutely splendid!" said the major, doing likewise.

"None better!" chipped in the captain, following suit, but dropping egg-yolk all down his medals.

"Our land has gone from strength to strength under your inspired leadership," said the colonel, reaching for a second egg.

"Oh, absolutely," agreed the major, swiping another.

"Indubitably," offered the captain, who added by way of explanation as the other two looked at him sharply, "Without a doubt." Then he, too, purloined another egg.

All the while, Mungo sat in a dreamy haze of cigar smoke, saying nothing, but lapping up every word of their smooth soft-talk. So rapt was he and so full of egg were the others that they never heard the hearthstone levered up, nor did they see three figures emerge with blogging-sticks at the ready. After the first three, the whole company of Great Beyonders came out, followed by Nero Squinks, who wanted to be first back into the hole in case anything went wrong.

But nothing did go wrong for them. The colonel was about to start hogging a box of chocolates when a blogging-stick came up behind him and he was biffed on the bonce. His outstretched hand never reached the chocolates. The major and the captain had just time to wonder why their colonel had suddenly gone quiet, when they joined him in dreamland, dropping silently on the thick carpet so that Mungo suspected nothing at first. His eyes were tightly closed, and he'd purred himself into an ecstasy listening to their non-stop flattery. The bloggers awaited his eye-opening.

He did so slowly, shifting uneasily in his chair, for the silence had begun to become oppressive. He drew on his cigar and said, "Well, you were about to say what we were going to do to the Domuslanders—and the Great Beyonders—when we've captured them. Oh, what would I give to see the faces of those poor fools now!" and he guffawed at the thought till his great, gold chain jingled noisily on the crests of his laugh.

"Open your eyes and your wish will be granted," said Horatio softly.

The chain stopped as suddenly as it had started. Bill Badger took the cat's cigar from his mouth for it drooped dangerously toward his paunch. The cat at last had had his eyes opened.

"You . . . how did? . . . where did? . . . who let you? . . ." he began. Then he saw the unconscious figures of his officers.

"We came up through the fires of your heart," explained Mack. "Through the dreams of your desires."

"Now are you going to come quietly," said Brushy, "or do we have to give you the gentle persuasion we gave these?" He pointed at the figures on the floor.

Mungo nodded dumbly. He was lost for words. He knew the game was up. So he simply nodded sadly and meekly followed them back down the secret stairs to the mineshaft.

"You never knew you had a secret passage under your house, did you?" said Nero. "Just think. You had a ready-made bolt-hole if you'd needed it. Everyone like you needs a bolt-hole, you know. You should have treated old Nero better, you should; you overfed, flea-bitten, mangy alley cat!"

And Nero's words were the unkindest cut Mungo had suffered for years. They took him back to the flying-machine, now painted to look like a Griptoe—and you'll find out why later. They entered it and fastened Mungo securely in the back seat. Then they set out for the entrance to the Tunnel at the Domusland end, to put into action the next stage of their plans.

Chapter 11

Guided by Nero Squinks, the animals went back through the winding shafts of the old lead-mines, until they reached the end of the Tunnel in Domusland. Meanwhile, at the other end in Wasteland, the army of rats had gathered ready to invade. They'd been up all night, cleaning their muskets and polishing their kit, ready for an inspection by President Mungo Brown—for he'd given himself his old title. However, things did not work out at all as they intended.

To begin with, Derry Dormouse had been told to scare the guards round Mungo's bungalow by telling them their leader had been snatched by fearsome creatures coming up through the floor. After he'd told them, the guards rushed in led by the young lieutenant. He stood aghast when he saw his colonel, major, and captain looking decidedly otherworldly as their eyes rolled round and round. He tried to get some sense out of them, shouting, "Wake up! Wake up! Please sir, what's happened?" But not an ounce of understanding could he extract. Someone had to take responsibility, and it fell on his young shoulders—not very broad, I'm afraid.

You see, he was a very young rat and had only just been made up to lieutenant. He'd no idea what to do. He turned and asked the nearest soldiers for advice, but they simply began chattering at once. Then one of them said they ought to ask Derry, as he'd been in the room when the 'things' had come.

"Good idea, my man. Good idea!" chirruped the lieutenant. "We really ought to find out exactly what happened and then *do* something. But, oh! how I wish the captain would wake up! I'm bound to make the wrong decision."

How right he was. It was the biggest mistake of his life asking Derry what had happened. Derry scratched his head and opened his eyes wide, then began telling them, in that slow, dor fashion, just what "terrible fearsome critters had sprung through the floor, right afore my fritted eyes!"

"I was a-standin' 'ere," he went on slowly. "An' they was a-standin' there, eatin' chocs an' eggs, when suddenly they come up!" And at this point he opened his eyes doubly wide, which set the soldiers gibbering and looking nervously all around them.

"They come up ..." gulped the officer, "wh ... where?"

Derry turned slowly to the fireplace and pointed. "Through the hearth," he whispered. "Ar—they come up through there. An' for ought I knows they may come up again."

The rats stepped back—toward the door—leaving Derry by himself in the middle of the room with the officers. Then he continued, "They they took Chairman Mungo with them sayin' he was the fattest 'an would keep best, like."

"B ... b ... but for goodness sake, who were *they*?" stammered the officer.

"I can't rightly say, sir," replied Derry, enjoying himself hugely. "I cleared out quick. But before I went, I hear Chairman Brown scream. He yelled summat about Griptoes an' Grozzies. Couldn't rightly make him out. But I dursen't look at 'em. They smelled so horrible an' the Chairman was screaming so . . ."

At the sound of Griptoes and Grozzies, the rats began quaking. One guard said, "We got to get 'elp!" But another said, "There's no 'elp against Griptoes and Grozzies." A third yammered, "Let's get out of 'ere before they grab us!" It was his suggestion they all followed.

They fled as fast as they could, rushing the door; but two fat rats jammed in the doorway, so that the lieutenant had to pound hard on their backs to get them through. "Let me go first! Let me go first!" he shouted. "I'm an officer! I must lead you out!" It was no good. They couldn't budge until with strength born of fear, he gave an extra mighty heave and they shot out of the doorway like corks from a bottle.

They landed in a heap, the officer and the two rats, but that didn't stop those behind. They poured out of the room, treading over the trio on the deck and running as fast as they could, shouting to all and sundry, "The Grozzies and Griptoes are on us! They've come through the floor and carried off Chairman Brown!" And what an effect that had. Once the other rats saw the dishevelled officer and his underlings belt out of the house two moments later, they took off as well.

"To the Tunnel!" someone shouted. "Let's get back to Wasteland!"

With that they threw down their arms and ran pell-mell—led by the officer. They reached the Tunnel before the Great Beyonders, who were moving slowly underground, and word went round that the Grozzies and Griptoes were about, on the rampage and looking for anyone to eat. That started wholesale panic. Black Jackets, soldiers, guards, police—the lot, all began to stampede down the Tunnel back to Wasteland.

The Great Beyonders saw them all milling back as they surfaced. "It worked!" croaked Kraken. "Derry's put the wind up 'em good an' proper. Show 'em the flying-machine an' turn on its engine to full roar. That should jolly 'em up even better."

They dragged the flying-machine with its painted face into the Tunnel and turned on its engines. Hoot revved them up full. My, how that shifted them! But there was more to come. " 'Ere," said Mack the Fat. "I just had another brainwave. Let's send old Nero after them—singing!"

"What a splendid idea," said Quill. "Only plug your ears first."

"You really mean it?" said Nero, greatly flattered. "You really want me to sing? Oh, goodie." And the rat lifted himself onto his toes to launch into song, there and then, but Mack clamped a wing over his mouth.

"Not yet," he said. "I haven't plugged up—an' I think it would also be a good idea if you takes Mungo back with you and explains what's happened. Your folk will know how to deal with him now he hasn't got his Black Jackets to guard him."

Then Mack plugged his ears, before handing over Mungo Brown, now tightly bound, for Nero to take back to gaol. Nero put a rope round the fat paunch and pulled away mightily, leading the miserable cat down the Tunnel, singing for all he was worth.

I couldn't begin to describe the effect his singing had further down the Tunnel, nor the torment it was for Mungo Brown who had to trudge after him listening to the hullabaloo—which had more 'baloo' than 'hulla' in it. It was terrible! It was downright wicked! Mungo was never the same cat after.

The odd rat or two who were scurrying down the Tunnel behind them stopped in their tracks, then turned and fled back to Domusland. There they threw themselves at the feet of the Great Beyonders begging for mercy rather than having to go up the Tunnel.

Later, when the last note of Squinks' singing had died away, the Great Beyonders went round freeing the imprisoned animals. Then all rats remaining on the wrong side of the Tunnel were herded together and sent packing back to Wasteland, carting their equipment with them. Ere long, every rodent had vanished from the land, under the Mystery Marshes. Once home, they joined the revolt against Mungo. He was imprisoned, along with his Black Jackets, and a new era dawned, as Mungo said it would; only it wasn't the era he'd imagined.

Serious efforts were made to clean up the land, led by Nero Squinks himself. They made him leader—on condition he promised never to sing. They even renamed Mungoville in his honour, and from that time on it was known as Squinkstown. Nero was its very first mayor, and he took his job very seriously. He had the public good truly at heart. He never publicly sang again, but he did continue privately in the old lead-mines, for he loved singing so much. After his practices he used to cross discreetly into Domusland from time to time to look up old friends there, including Mack and Mick.

And the Tunnel, what became of that? Well, when the very last rat had gone home, the Great Beyonders were invited to the Black Wood Moot to decide what was to be done with it. Eldermouse Derry Dor chaired the meeting, in which many important laws were passed. No Domuslander was allowed to sell his land to strangers, and no more horrid roads or buildings were constructed. Many, indeed, were demolished, and trees grew once more in Old Coppice. In a few years, there remained no sign at all of Mungo's evil plans to build towns and housing estates.

Finally, when the Tunnel was cleared of folk, the Wasteland end of it was sealed. Hoot spent an entire day drilling holes and planting dynamite with one of his robots. When they'd done, it was ready for the Big Bang. Crouching behind a handy hummock, Hoot and his friends ignited the dynamite.

Nothing was heard for a second, then a distant rumbling began, far away under the Mystery Marshes. Wasteland children thought that Grozzies and Griptoes were on the move and ran indoors to hide their heads in their mothers' aprons. But Wastelanders living on the hills overlooking the marshes saw a huge whirlpool begin to form. Faster and faster it swirled as gallons of water and mud poured into the Tunnel. It was like the plug being taken from some gigantic bath. Eventually the whirlpool began to slow down. Then it ceased. A few giant bubbles plopped to the surface and that was that. The Tunnel was no more.

Three hearty cheers for the Great Beyonders went up in Domusland. There followed a civic dinner which lasted well into the night, with the Great Beyonders as chief guests. Then next day, they climbed into the flying-machine after shaking hands all round. On its side was a newly painted emblem—a black raven, which made old Kraken swell with pride. He, Dink, and Quill waved and waved till the Great Beyonders were out of sight, then returned to their old life in the Meadow.

However, in Black Wood things weren't quite the same. Two new policemen were appointed to keep a better eye on things. They're still there; one of them exceedingly fat and going bald, the other now respectably plump. They are P.C. Mick and Police Sergeant Mack Magpie, and very efficient policemen they are, too. Always one jump ahead of would-be law-breakers. They ought to be, for they are past-masters at that trade! So good are they, in fact, that they solve every case of burglary, which is a lost art in Domusland now.

Your Nature Diary

_____

_____

_____

_____

_____

_____

_____

_____

_____

_____

_____

_____

_____

_____

Join the
Quill Hedgehog Club

Quill and his friends invite you to join their Quill Hedgehog Club and receive the latest exciting news from Hedgehog Corner.
When you become a member of the club, you will receive a *membership certificate*, a *Hedgehog Club badge*, and *Quill's Club Newsletter*, which is issued four times a year.

You will be among the very first to learn about Quill and his friends' newest adventures and their battles to protect the environment.

To join, just send your name and address and $10.00 to:

Quill Hedgehog
Hedgehog Corner
Fair View, Old Coppice
Lyth Bank
Shrewsbury
Shropshire
England SY3 0BW

from John Muir Publications

The Quill Hedgehog Adventure Series

*I*n our first series of green fiction for young readers, Quill Hedgehog, an ardent environmentalist, and his animalfolk friends battle such foes as the villainous alley cat Mungo Brown, the Wasteland rats, and the Grozzies.

Quill's Adventures in the Great Beyond
Book One
John Waddington-Feather
5½" × 8½", 96 pages, $5.95 paper

Quill's Adventures in Wasteland
Book Two
John Waddington-Feather
5½" × 8½", 132 pages, $5.95 paper

Quill's Adventures in Grozzieland
Book Three
John Waddington-Feather
5½" × 8½", 132 pages, $5.95 paper

The Extremely Weird Series

*F*ew things of the imagination are as amazing or as weird as the wonders that Mother Nature produces, and that's the idea behind our Extremely Weird series. Each title is filled with full-size, full-color photographs and descriptions of the extremely weird thing depicted.

Extremely Weird Bats
Text by Sarah Lovett
8½" × 11", 48 pages, $9.95 paper

Extremely Weird Frogs
Text by Sarah Lovett
8½" × 11", 48 pages, $9.95 paper

Extremely Weird Spiders
Text by Sarah Lovett
8½" × 11", 48 pages, $9.95 paper

Extremely Weird Primates
Text by Sarah Lovett
8½" × 11", 48 pages, $9.95

Extremely Weird Reptiles
Text by Sarah Lovett
8½" × 11", 48 pages, $9.95

The Kids' Environment Series

*T*he titles in this series, all of which are printed on recycled paper, examine the environmental issues and opportunities that kids will face during their lives. They suggest ways young people can become involved and thoughtful citizens of planet Earth.

Rads, Ergs, and Cheeseburgers
The Kids' Guide to Energy and the Environment
Bill Yanda
Illustrated by Michael Taylor
7" × 9", 108 pages, two-color illustrations, $12.95 paper

The Kids' Environment Book
What's Awry and Why
Anne Pedersen
Illustrated by Sally Blakemore
7" × 9", 192 pages, two-color illustrations, $13.95 paper
For Ages 10 and Up

The Indian Way
Learning to Communicate with Mother Earth
Gary McLain
Paintings by Gary McLain
Illustrations by Michael Taylor
7" × 9", 114 pages, two-color illustrations, $9.95 paper